Anything for You

Sweet Haven Farm Book Four

Jessie Gussman

Published By: Jessie Gussman

Contents

Acknowledgments

Editing by Heather Hayden
Narration by Jay Dyess
Author Services by CE Author Assistant

Listen to a FREE professionally performed and produced audio-book version of this title on Youtube. Search for "Say With Jay" to browse all available FREE Dyess/Gussman audiobooks.

Chapter 1

The words elephant and wedding really didn't belong in the same sentence.

Even if the wedding in question was being held in a barn.

At least, that was Jillian Powell's experience. But what did she know? She spent most of her life in the Mexican circus where the word elephant and pretty much any other word in English or Spanish would have been perfectly normal. Possibly mundane, even.

At her current location, in central Pennsylvania at the wedding of her good friend and dubious relation, Avery Williams, though, elephant definitely did not fit.

"What did you say that noise was again?" Avery leaned over and whispered in Jillian's ear.

The brass ensemble that had been playing in the background while the guests had started eating had taken a break. The low murmurs of the guests had jerked into stunned silence when Heidi, the elephant, had trumpeted just a few seconds ago.

Jillian's palms started to sweat and her heart shivered like leaves that had been blown from a baobab tree by the lonely and sad trumpet of an African bush elephant.

"It's Heidi," Jillian whispered back, surprised her voice only shook a little. Heidi and her sister, Hazel, had been part of Jillian's act when she'd been in the Mexican circus. Not that she was going to go into her history with the elephant that currently stood below them in the long-unused barnyard.

That wasn't exactly the most pressing question on anyone's mind, anyway. 'How did the elephant get here, might be the top question in most peoples' minds.

Jillian, however, was more concerned about the best man.

No, she wasn't attracted to McKoy Rodning, although with his square jaw, strong nose, and broad shoulders, he probably was attractive. Maybe she did spend more than the average amount of time thinking about him. Only because of her recently opened dog kennel. Or maybe because of her general distrust of government employees.

But her current level of apprehension stemmed from the fact that McKoy Rodning was the animal control officer, and it was pretty much his job to question why an elephant would be trumpeting, independent of the brass band, at Avery and Gator's wedding.

And there she had it. Elephant and wedding in the same sentence, once more, sounding no more harmonious than they had the first time.

"And you know...Heidi?" Avery whispered, the pucker between her brows not matching the bright smile she flashed the curious guests who had slowly started conversing in low tones, throwing occasional concerned glances up at the wedding party table.

"Yes." Jillian rubbed her wet palms together, trying to remember she was wearing satin and not denim, and could not wipe her hands down her legs like she longed to do. Hopefully, the sweat that gathered in her armpits wasn't noticeable as long as she kept her arms pressed firmly against her sides.

The musicians began filing back to their seats. Avery pushed her half-eaten piece of cake away from the edge of the table and gave Jillian a nervous smile.

"If you leave before this dance, it will be noticeable, but I think once it ends, you could slip out and take care of whatever you need to. Maybe I can get Gator to distract McKoy."

"You two just enjoy each other. I can handle it." It's not like she hadn't learned plenty of survival skills growing up in the circus. Although how one would "take care" of an elephant problem in central Pennsylvania presented a quagmire she wasn't sure her skill set could handle.

Avery squeezed her hand, her shiny pink nails sparkling in the romantic barn light. "Thank you. Thank you for spending this day with me."

Jillian's smile was genuine as she squeezed back. Avery had been a great friend to her.

"Guess this is where I try not to step on your toes," Gator spoke, and Avery's head swiveled to him.

He had stood and held his hand out to her, his eyes full of love and admiration, even if his request to dance had been less than romantic. His jeans and plaid shirt looked new, though they weren't typical groom attire. They suited the barn wedding, and they suited Gator even more.

Just as the lacy white dress suited Avery.

Unfortunately, the coral satin dress Jillian wore might look fabulous next to her brown skin and black eyes and hair, but she would feel slightly more comfortable in a bikini standing at the South Pole than she currently did in the dress and the four-inch heels.

She wore outfits like this when she performed in the circus. Well, maybe not with the full skirt that fell below her knees. But definitely with heels this high. She could hold a hoop for the dog act, hang by her hair above the audience, twist herself into a pretzel, perch a monkey on her shoulder and ride the lead elephant's trunk around the show ring with no more nervousness than if she were sitting in bed, reading a book.

But somehow she felt she needed the security of comfortable jeans, worn sneakers, and a soft T-shirt to face Mr. McKoy Rodning, animal control officer and the only one currently in attendance at this wedding who had the power to remove Heidi before Jillian could figure out where she came from, who brought her, and what she was going to do with her. If he knew the secret that her hosts, the Finkenbinders, didn't know...Avery didn't even know...he could have her sent back to Mexico.

But she didn't have the security of comfortable clothes and he stood beside her, one hand behind his back, one hand held out to her, bowing slightly. The manners in his posture were impeccable, but the look in those powerful blue eyes was speculating.

Their relationship was not exactly harmonious.

They didn't belong in the same dance together any more than elephant and wedding belonged in the same sentence.

With a lift of her chin and a glint of her own eye, she met the challenge in his gaze, placing her hand in his.

Like sticking her fingers in a light socket.

Jillian fought to hold steady as shockwaves ricocheted up her arm, past her elbow, and slammed into her shoulder.

Her eyes flew to his, even as her automatic brain took over and her performing smile slid easily into place on her face. The net might have broken, but she would smile all the way to the ground.

Her fingers, long and slender like the rest of her body, rested lightly in his large, calloused hand.

The touch was light, but that crazy electricity that zapped between them felt stronger than the poles that held the big top up.

Her performance mask solidified on her face.

"Thank you," she said as she rose gracefully.

Something flickered in his eye as she straightened to her full height, her eyes square with his chin. Her stomach jumped in answer. Nervousness. It had to be. Had he recognized that noise for what it was?

He led her to the dance area, where Avery and Gator already danced to the dulcet tones of the brass ensemble.

She'd have to distract him so he wouldn't ask about the noise. But how? All she knew about McKoy she'd heard from the town gossips. He was the "dog catcher." Straight-laced. Followed the law to the T. Solid. Dependable. Still lived in the house he grew up in. Boring.

She could try to talk about stocks and bonds. That sounded boring enough to suit his personality. Except she couldn't hold even a remotely intelligent conversation about that. Maybe he was the kind of man who dominated conversations and tried to show by his verbosity how erudite he was.

It was too much to chance.

He stopped and she turned, her skirt billowing out, brushing his leg. Something about the soft satin of her skirt brushing the rough denim of his pant leg mesmerized her, and she watched as the material seemed to flow, smooth as cream over strawberries, across his strong leg.

She'd been required to do a lot of things in her time as a performer, but talking wasn't one of them. Her brain seemed to freeze as his large hand came up to settle with a whisper on her waist.

His lips didn't turn up, and he looked as serious as a pallbearer at a funeral. Apparently he wasn't any more eager to dance with her than she was with him. She'd just opened a dog kenneling business here on the farm, and so far he'd left her alone, but that didn't mean he wouldn't be visiting.

All of her paperwork was in order. Her business paperwork. Fink, who owned the farm with his wife Ellie, had filed it for her.

Her personal paperwork, on the other hand, was nonexistent. From what she'd heard of McKoy, he wouldn't hesitate to turn her in, but he shouldn't have any idea that she wasn't legal, unless she managed to stuff her high heel in her mouth in the next three minutes. Because of the different nationalities in the circus, she'd grown up speaking four different languages—Slovak, Romanian, Spanish, and English. Her Slovak and Romanian were rusty, but she was fluent in the other two languages. She'd been told her accent was faint.

Would he notice?

All of her upbringing had been focused on giving the audience a performance that made them feel their money was well-spent. It was time to put her talent to use.

He tilted his head, as though listening, then opened his mouth. He was going to ask about that noise, she was sure of it. She had to speak first. She had to distract him.

"Did you know that all monarch butterflies winter in one general area in Mexico?"

His mouth froze halfway open. His brows slowly formed a V, and if she read the look in his eyes correctly, he had just decided she was eccentric, if not slightly nuts. Perfect. He wasn't thinking about elephants anymore.

"It's beautiful to visit in the winter and see them almost covering every tree or bush within that certain square mile or two."

He blinked.

The circus had been playing a week-long show near the mountain on which the butterflies spent the winter, and she'd gone with her mother and several others to see it. "There's a lot of deforestation going on near that area, and scientists are afraid the monarchs will lose their home."

"Surely Mexico has laws in place to prevent that from happening," McKoy said with typical American naivete. Americans thought Mexico was like America.

"In Mexico, the person with the biggest bribe wins." She remembered just in time she wasn't supposed to sound bitter.

"Sounds like a nice vacation," he said. Ignoring the uncomfortable idea that monarchs might become extinct. Not surprising.

They swayed gently to the music. McKoy wasn't trying any fancy dance moves, which fitted exactly what she'd heard about his personality. He seemed uncomfortable in front of the guests, too.

She'd exhausted her monarch trivia, and he had that look in his eye, like he might be asking about the noise that had sounded suspiciously like an elephant trumpeting.

McKoy might not be her favorite person, but normally she wouldn't purposely do something that made someone uncomfortable. For Heidi, she felt she had no choice.

"Did I tell you I used to be a dancer?"

It was a rhetorical question, since they'd never spoken before five minutes ago.

He shook his head, his mouth still slightly open.

She gave him a little smile that might have had just a hint of deviltry in it. "I'm going to spin. Hang on."

A look very close to panic flashed across his face before she moved, grabbing his hand and stretching out their arms, then spinning herself up next to him. Their faces were only inches apart before she spun out, bending backward. She wasn't quite as flexible as she used to be, and her head was less than a foot off the ground, rather than the mere inches it would have been in her circus days.

The guests clapped.

She straightened slowly and twirled under his arm, turning completely around several times. Her skirt billowed out, but she refused to acknowledge it brushing his jeans. It wasn't herself she was trying to distract.

This time, as she twirled into him, he caught her, probably on accident, with his arm around her waist.

Her unconventional childhood had also taught her never to waste an opportunity.

She bent over his arm, careful not to lift her leg up too high. She hadn't been expecting this and her undergarments were not sufficient for *that* kind of show.

The song faded out on a low chord, she bent backward one last time, seeing Avery and Gator smiling before they kissed. The guests clapped.

She straightened.

McKoy offered his arm, which surprised her for some reason. His cheeks were red under his tan, and he didn't look her in the eye as she took it and he led her back to her seat.

She'd been trained since birth to be in complete control of her body at all times. So McKoy would never guess when she tripped and spilled the punch sitting on her table down the front of her dress that it wasn't an accident.

"Oh, no!" Jillian said with a glance at Avery and Gator, who were oblivious, wrapped up in each other's arms. "I'd better go blot this so the stain doesn't set."

She had plenty of experience in the circus of sewing costumes and getting stains out, and it didn't matter how much "blotting" she did, that stain was never coming out of her dress. But she was willing to sacrifice her pretty bridesmaid dress on the altar of saving Heidi.

McKoy jerked his head up and stepped back so she could go around him.

The restrooms in the renovated barn were around the corner at the far end in what used to be granaries. There were no windows in the small single user bathrooms, but there was a window at the end of the hall between them.

Jillian opened it, hitched her dress up, and climbed out.

Chapter 2

McKoy pulled his shirt sleeves down and adjusted the cuffs at the end of his wrists. It wasn't a task that required his eyes, and they stayed hooked on Jillian as she walked away. Floated away, was more like it. He'd never met a more graceful woman.

Funny how that glass of punch seemed to jump up onto her dress.

He grabbed several napkins off the table and blotted up the few drops that had made it to the ground, trying to get his breathing under control while waiting for his brain to wake up from whatever spell the woman had put it under. He'd never been so bewitched by a lady in all his life. Monarch butterflies. Backbends as graceful as a ballerina. And he, a clumsy clod whose sole purpose throughout the dance was trying to breathe and avoid stepping on her toes.

He kept his face toward the restrooms, watching for Jillian to come back out.

The few times he'd seen her, her black eyes had always regarded him suspiciously. But today it seemed like she was hiding something.

Then she'd deliberately tried to dazzle him with her supple grace and amazing dance moves. It had worked. To a point. He was just like any other man when a beautiful woman draped herself over his arm.

At least he figured he was. Not that beautiful women were rushing to drape themselves over his arms. But in theory.

Funny, because Jillian had gone out of her way to avoid him every other time they'd gotten within twenty feet of each other.

So, yeah. He was pretty sure she hadn't all of a sudden developed a thing for him.

Maybe she just liked to dance. Couldn't be fun dancing with someone like him, who had two left feet that didn't know how to do much more than shuffle around the floor. She had enough talent for both of them.

Two teen girls whose family owned and bred rotties on the other side of Love, the nearest town to Sweet Haven Farm, giggled as they went down the hall to the restroom. There was only one room for ladies, so Jillian would be hurrying back soon.

He'd keep his eye on her when she did. The woman was hiding something. His job had taught him to recognize all the tells.

"There's that big, strong dog catcher," Mrs. Paulson exclaimed as she hobbled over, her walker clacking in front of her.

He hated it when people called him the dog catcher. He did a lot more than round up strays. But he couldn't get upset with Mrs. Paulson. She'd paid him to mow her grass when he was younger—his first job. Plus, she was a friend of his mother's.

"I want to dance with you." Mrs. Paulson clinked to a stop in front of him.

"Let me help you, Mrs. Paulson." He offered his hand as she settled her walker off to the side.

Telling her no wasn't an option. But he could keep his face pointed at the restrooms.

The band started up, a brisk, upbeat song. Mrs. Paulson was eighty if she was a day, and McKoy couldn't dance worth squat, so he could see this ending badly, but he gamely stood while Mrs. Paulson put her arms around his waist. He put his hands on her shoulders. The faint scent of eucalyptus oil mixed with spaghetti sauce drifted up to his nose. Her white hair swayed in the breeze as she leaned on him and did an old-lady type hop.

"My Billy knew how to tear up the dance floor," Mrs. Paulson shouted over the music.

McKoy nodded. He wasn't much of a shouter. Couldn't dance, didn't shout. Maybe Isabella, his ex-fiancée, had been right when she'd called him boring. That had been a little over ten years ago. Before they were out of college. She'd spent their junior year in Germany.

She'd taken his engagement ring with her. But she'd left it in a pawn shop in Paris after meeting a big, blond German dude who looked a lot like McKoy, although their bank accounts didn't have anything in common.

McKoy had figured it boiled down to money and didn't pay much attention to the boring comment.

Not true. For the last ten years, he'd pretty much given up on impressing a girl, since his idea of a good time was sitting on his front porch with his uncle who'd raised him and watching the sun go down. A really exciting evening might have them doing that while eating ice cream.

Jillian would consider him boring.

He wasn't sure where that rogue thought came from, but he squashed it. He didn't give a fig what Jillian thought.

Just then the two teens who had gone to the restroom came back out the hall, their heads still bent together, laughing.

McKoy's eyes scanned the barn floor. Jillian was not among the guests.

Mrs. Paulson did an extra high hop and landed on his cowboy boot. His lip twitched, but he managed not to flinch while he tightened his grip on her shoulders until she caught her balance. Thankfully her orthopedic shoes were flat-soled.

"Oh, sonny! I'm sorry." She squeezed his waist. "It's so nice to have a strong man to hold onto."

He wasn't real interested in holding onto any man, strong or otherwise. "I'll take your word for it."

"Huh?" Her head swiveled up and she squinted at him. "What did you say?"

"Okay." He didn't yell, but he did try to give an extra punch to his words. Where was Jillian? And what was she hiding?

She'd opened a dog kennel in the last few months. Because of his job, how he travelled all over, he knew most of the gossip in town. Word of mouth said the place was clean and well-run. McKoy wouldn't expect anything less of a business under Fink's direction. But it was his job to do an inspection, and he'd be getting around to it soon.

The song ended, mercifully. They hadn't moved too far from their little corner of the dance floor and McKoy helped Mrs. Paulson shuffle back to her walker.

"I'm not as flashy as your previous partner, but it was nice of you to give an old lady a few minutes and a nice dance."

McKoy nodded and Mrs. Paulson shuffled off.

A hand clamped on his shoulder. "Thanks for standing up with me," Gator said.

"It was my honor." McKoy turned and shook the proffered hand. "Happy to do it."

"Yeah. I know you probably had a hundred other things you could have done today, but I appreciate it."

"Wish you the best, man," McKoy said.

"We're cutting out. Just wanted to let you know."

McKoy grinned. "Better git. Don't want to miss a second of that wedding night."

Gator flashed a grin of his own, even as his eyes sought out his bride, standing over by his mother. "I don't think she's going to leave without me."

"Where you going?" McKoy asked. They'd spent some time together before the wedding, but they'd not talked about honeymoons.

"Montana. We're spending the week there. My mom's done with her treatments, and the doctors say no cancer, so now is the time to go."

"I can check on your mom, if you'd like."

"That would ease my mind some. Jillian will be stopping in, too. She and Avery usually take food over when I have to be gone."

He wasn't excited about running into Jillian. But, speaking of... "Do you know where Jillian went?"

Gator's gaze skidded away. "That was some dance you two had."

"I didn't figure you took your eyes off Avery long enough to have any idea of what the rest of the world was doing."

Gator laughed and slapped McKoy on the back. "I'll see you in a few weeks or so. Avery has a wedding to coordinate here next week, so we'll be around."

"Have a great time," McKoy called after him.

With one more glance around the rustically decorated barn, McKoy moved over along the wall and walked to the restroom. He turned the corner of the hall. The bathroom door hung open. Empty.

It was a dead end.

But the window was cracked.

McKoy strode quickly down the hall and to the window. Too high. No way someone could go out and survive that fall. He pushed the window down and locked it before turning and peering in both bathrooms. Dark and empty.

He could have missed Jillian. Maybe when Mrs. Paulson stepped on his toe?

But his gut was telling him he wasn't wrong. That Jillian was up to something. And she wasn't on the barn floor with the rest of the guests.

Moving back out of the hall, he looked around as he came to the big open room. Lights that looked like lanterns hung from the ceiling, along with greenery and some kind of white flower. It was a tall ladder that would have gotten up to those rafters where the lights were strung.

The brass instruments were playing a popular tune and the guests were laughing and clapping. Gator and Avery were gone. Jillian still wasn't there.

McKoy slipped behind the chairs and tables and out the side door into the chill of late winter. Spring was a few weeks away. The patches of snow, like islands in a brown sea, were getting smaller and smaller.

He hardly paid attention to the melting snow as he strode around the side of the barn. It was late afternoon, and the sun had almost nestled on the top of the mountain.

He was snooping. No other word for it. But his gut was never wrong.

Faint barks came from on down the hill where a low building, surrounded by chain link fence, sat beside a large field of Christmas trees. He could see a couple of large dogs running out of their dog doors, barking and running back in.

None of the animals were tethered, and they all looked healthy. He was sure that everything was code, but he'd be around to check.

Rounding the corner of the barn, he went down a steep hill and came to a long metal gate. He paused and listened.

He thought he could hear a voice, soft and low.

The memory of Jillian's voice, sweet and lyrical, with a hint of some accent he couldn't trace, brought an unexpected longing to his soul. He shook his head. Her crazy talk about butterflies, of all things. She gave new meaning to the definition of small talk. Weren't they supposed to talk about the weather?

At least she hadn't talked about the latest TV shows. He wouldn't have been able to say as much as he had.

Unlatching the chain that held the gate shut, he opened it and slipped inside, closing and latching it behind him, cognizant of the number one rule of farm living: close the gate.

The barnyard was muddy, and he stepped carefully, trying to keep his good boots from getting ruined. The talking came a little clearer and louder.

Suddenly, an ear-killing noise rent the air around him. He wasn't expecting it, and he actually started to duck, although he'd never been in a war zone.

He'd also never heard an elephant trumpet in real time. But he'd watched enough documentaries that he was pretty sure that's what it was. Except he was under a barn in central Pennsylvania and elephants weren't native to any state in the union.

Pythons had invaded the everglades.

The climate wasn't right for elephants.

It came again.

This time McKoy didn't duck, but the sound made his ears ring.

"Would you please stop? You're scaring her."

He peered into the deeper gloom of the area under the barn, where her voice, soft and husky, with just a trace of a faint accent he couldn't place, came from.

His eyes needed a minute to adjust. Eventually, he distinguished Jillian's face out of the gloom, and that bright coral dress. The one that made her complexion glow. That contrasted with her black hair and snapping black eyes, making them shine.

Nothing was shining in the gloom, but Jillian's irritation almost crackled.

Eventually he could see eyes, way up toward the ceiling, and one tusk.

"Holy smokes." It was much bigger than he might have expected an elephant to be. "That really is an elephant."

Jillian put her hand on the beast's trunk, between her eyes, and spoke low and soft.

A shaft of fear split through McKoy's backbone. "You'd better get back. I've heard they can be unpredictable and of course, they're strong."

"I have experience with elephants."

"Oh?" His shock faded and questions, legal questions, started whirling through his mind.

"I worked in a circus for a lot of years."

Ah, maybe she picked up her accent from fellow performers who were from a different country.

He nodded at the beast. "Is this your elephant?"

His eyes had gotten more accustomed to the gloom, and he could see her hesitation. The way her hand stopped rubbing the elephant's nose. The way she bit her lip. She shifted. "Yes."

Hmm. Something off there.

"You have a permit?" He'd have to brush up on the actual law, since, although he was the animal control officer for this area, he'd never dealt specifically with a privately housed elephant before.

"No?" she said. "Do I need a permit?"

"Yes, of course you do." He tried to sound like he knew what he was talking about, since it was his job, after all, although he was completely faking it, since he didn't really have a clue. Still, while there were differences between the types of animals and specific regulations, most "exotic" animals required a permit and certain space and water specifications.

"I'll get one," she murmured.

"How long have you had it?" Funny that Gator hadn't mentioned it.

"It just got dropped off today." She dropped her hand from the elephant's face and stepped toward him. He felt like she was trying to get him to back up.

He crossed his arms over his chest. Technically he was off duty, but this was definitely something he needed to check out.

If he wanted that promotion that was coming up, he'd better not let a little thing like an unpermitted elephant exist right under his nose. If his co-worker, Todd, found out about it, he'd be telling their boss, and the promotion almost certainly would go to Todd. The promotion meant more money, sure, but it also meant less travel and no overnight work trips. He'd be able to keep his uncle in his house rather than having him move to a senior living center.

"I can give you thirty days, but you'll need to have a permit by then."

"I will." Her voice was confident, lilting and stirred the pleasure sensors in his ears. Interesting, since he hadn't even known that he had pleasure centers in his ears until he'd heard Jillian speak.

She took another step forward. She still wore the heels she'd danced in. Her dress shimmered around her legs. All of it looked out of place in the dingy barnyard.

"Do you know what they eat?" he asked, his voice sounding gruff.

"Yes."

"Can you afford to feed it?" That's where people seemed to get into trouble. Everyone thought it would be cool to own a boa or tiger or some other exotic animal, but they didn't figure in the expense of providing food for such a creature. It didn't even have to be an exotic animal. He'd seen plenty of horses whose owners hadn't considered how much they needed to eat.

Another lip bite and eye shift. "Yes."

From her reaction, he believed she really did know what they ate, and knew it was going to be expensive. "What do they eat?"

"They eat grass. I could feed her hay. Straw, even. I can get shavings from the mill."

She seemed to be talking in future tense, which he found odd. "So you have some food for her tonight?"

"I promise she'll be taken care of. Why don't you go back and enjoy the reception, and I'll deal with Heidi.."

He stood with his hands on his hips. She'd just basically ordered him out. He really didn't have a leg to stand on until he was here in an official capacity. He didn't want to make an enemy. But the elephant had to be his first concern.

"Can I help you?" he asked.

Yeah, she wasn't expecting that. Her brows shot way up and her red lips parted. He snapped his eyes away from her lips.

"She's upset and scared. I think it's best if I do it."

"How'd she get here?"

"I don't know."

He tilted his head. "You don't know?"

She sighed and looked away. "I know that sounds weird, but it's true. I wasn't expecting her, I don't know how she got here, and I don't know who brought her or why. But I'm sure this is Heidi, one of two sister elephants that I worked with in the circus."

The tip of a gray trunk felt around Jillian's neck, coming out from under the hair that lay in limp curls on her shoulders.

McKoy's breath caught in his lungs. "Hold still. I'll distract it while you move away."

"What?" Her hand reached up and she took the trunk in her hand, stroking with her other. "She's scared and doesn't want me to leave her. She and her sister, Hazel, never left each other's sides. It's very weird to me that she's here alone." Her teeth bit down on her lip again. "I'm actually worried about Hazel."

"I might be able to put a few feelers out, but Heidi is the one that's here and she's the one we need to feed yet, tonight." His eyes had been telling him for the last few minutes that the light was fading. The brass ensemble still played above them and probably would be for another hour before McKoy had to go and help clean up.

"I can do it," Jillian insisted. She'd caught his subtle use of "we" and made sure to correct him.

So she was scared of his "official" capacity. Lots of people were. Like seeing a cop sitting along the road made everyone hit the brakes whether they were speeding or not.

"I'm not out to get you. As long as you get a permit in thirty days, and submit to one scheduled inspection and one unscheduled inspection per week, things will be just fine." He did have some experience with that protocol—the one where they made the inspections. He'd done it twice. Once with a guy who had a snake with no permit and once with a man who had a wolf.

Which reminded him. "Where are the papers for her?"

"What papers?" Her eyes got big.

"However they brought her, she should have come with papers."

"I'm sorry. I just found her maybe ten minutes before the wedding started. I haven't had time to look for papers. Maybe they're at the house."

He shoved a hand in his jeans pocket and hooked the other one around his neck. "I'll tell you what. I'll wait to examine the papers until the first inspection. Now, how about we get her a drink and something to eat, and we'll get her settled for the night?"

Her nose wrinkled and her cheeks tucked in like she was biting the insides of them.

He pulled out a pack of gum and held a piece out. "Here. Give your lips and cheeks a break and chew on this."

Her brows lifted, and her eyes shifted from the gum to his face before she gave a little, very little, laugh. "Okay. Thanks."

"Now. Will Fink and Ellie mind if you use some of that baled hay over there?" He pointed to a stack of hay in the corner. It looked as old as time, but hay, once baled, didn't go bad as long as it didn't get wet.

"Yes, I'm sure I can use whatever is here."

"Okay, then. Are you keeping her back there? I'll carry a few bales back."

"This is where I found her, so I think we should feed her here. I'll have to do something else about water."

He made two trips, carrying a bale in each hand both times by pulling the strings together, a trick he'd learned from summers spent helping neighbors bale hay. Then he dragged a metal trough back as far as he could before going to look for hoses and water. There were animals kept down here before, a long time ago, apparently, but it was a given there was water somewhere.

He found the spicket. And old, ratty-looking hose lay curled up beside it. He wasn't surprised when the hose leaked after he twisted it in and turned the spicket on.

But enough water came out of the hose to start filling the tank, which, thankfully, didn't leak.

While he was working, he kept an eye on Jillian. She moved in graceful, easy movements around the elephant, confident and unafraid. It wasn't hard to believe her that she'd worked with elephants before.

As long as she got the permit, everything should be fine.

Chapter 3

The man wouldn't leave.

He was actually a help, if Jillian were being honest. But she wanted to run her hands over Heidi, checking her and making sure she was okay. She wanted to get her cell phone and call David, her cousin who owned the zoo in Mexico where Heidi and Hazel went when the circus dissolved.

She needed to call Carlos, the man who could supply her with whatever fake papers she needed. Whoever brought Heidi probably didn't have papers. Nothing legit, anyway. Mexicans didn't always understand American's endless need for reams of paper, nor their need to constantly prove legality of something.

The water trough was almost full, and she opened her mouth to ask McKoy to shut it off, but he was already moving.

She ran her hand over Heidi's rough skin. "Come on, sweetheart. I'm sure you're thirsty."

She splashed the water a little, not much, lest Heidi think they were playing the splashing game. "It's too cold here most of the time to do that." Heidi loved the sound of her voice, so she spoke just to keep her calm.

She was definitely going to have to talk to Fink and Ellie tonight after the barn was cleaned up. After McKoy left. She had too many secrets for her to be getting buddy-buddy with a government worker. Especially one that played by the rules.

He came back and stood with his hands on his hips. It wasn't right for a man to smell as good as he did. Some kind of earthy, spicy, masculine scent that twisted her insides. Her brow furrowed.

Maybe a little eucalyptus oil in there too. Which was weird, since she hadn't caught that earlier when they were dancing.

"I appreciate your help," she said, and tried not to sound as grudging as she felt.

"It's obvious you've worked with elephants," he said. Was that the first nice thing he'd said to her?'

"For almost twenty years." She bit her tongue. She didn't want him to dig too deeply into her background.

"In the circus?"

"Yes."

"Which one?"

"A small, family circus."

He waited.

She wasn't going to speak to fill the silence, so he could just keep on waiting.

He gave up first. "I'm going back up. I'm on clean-up duty. That'll be starting here soon."

"I have the same duty." She hadn't thought he'd be helping, but she should have known. "I'll be up shortly."

"Be careful. It's getting dark." Like she couldn't see.

He hesitated. Maybe he didn't want to leave her alone, but he finally turned and left, to her relief. The dog catcher was not her friend.

She didn't have her normal ladder to reach the spot above Heidi's ears that she loved to have scratched, and Heidi wasn't wearing her bright pink harness that Jillian could grab and use to climb up. But it wasn't hard to find a pole she could climb. Kicking off her heels, she scaled it easily. It was a little trickier to hold the overhead beam with her hands and toes and work herself backward until she was over Heidi.

Letting go with her feet, she slowly settled onto Heidi's back and, letting go of the beam and leaning forward, scratched her ears.

Her dress was ruined, no doubt.

"Who brought you? And why?" she whispered. "How'd they get you here? And what am I supposed to do with you? Not that I'm not thrilled that you're here. I've missed you so much."

But she didn't have the money to feed an elephant. She didn't have the money to feed herself. Everything she was making was going to pay the coyote who facilitated her passage across the border. It didn't matter that she'd almost died in the desert. She still owed him several thousand dollars. And she still owed Carlos a cool three grand for bringing her up and getting her "papers"—a fake social security card and a fake work visa. They weren't real, but they were all she had.

Her mother always said her father was an American. Jillian believed it, since she got her height from her father's side of the family, and her mother had given her his last name—Powell. So, technically, she was a dual citizen—of Mexico and America. But her father wasn't listed on her birth certificate. So even though she should be an American citizen, she wasn't. Not with the missing name.

Which stunk. Because she'd almost bet the farm that in order to get a permit for Heidi, she needed to be a "real" citizen.

An hour later she'd changed into clean jeans and boots, thrown her hair into a ponytail, and had bolstered her courage to work alongside McKoy. Ellie and Fink and their kids would be there, so he probably wouldn't grill her.

She wasn't going to mention Heidi until after McKoy left. Hopefully he'd not mention her either.

But, no such luck. She walked into the barn where a few guests still milled about. The musicians were packing things up. McKoy and Fink had their heads bent together and were deep in conversation.

Her lips pressed together. Maybe they were talking about something different, but she somehow doubted it.

She greeted some of her friends and neighbors on her way over to where Fink and McKoy stood, and stopped to talk to several.

It was a good twenty minutes until she made it across the room in time to hear Fink say, "Well, I don't know what we're going to do with it."

She put her hands on her hips. Her chest felt hot. Why couldn't McKoy have kept his mouth shut?

"How about you let me figure that out?" She glared at McKoy so he'd have no doubt about how she felt about him.

Both men's heads tuned slowly toward her. They stared.

Something that felt an awful lot like a container of night crawlers squirmed in her stomach.

"You weren't talking about the elephant, were you?" she asked in a much less assertive tone.

Fink's brows shot up, almost smacking into the lights that were hanging from the ceiling.

McKoy's lip pulled back. "No," he said. "We weren't."

"Oh."

"We," Fink emphasized the "we," looking at McKoy, "were talking about the resort that we are going to begin construction on. We're waiting on one more permit, and when Avery and Gator come back, we're going to break ground."

McKoy crossed his arms over his chest. He was almost smirking.

"And I don't know what we're going to do with the dirt we're going to have to move," Fink finished. "Now. What's this about an elephant?"

Jillian pursed her lips. She hadn't wanted to talk about it now, but she was the one who'd just put her foot in her mouth.

"One of the elephants I used to work with at the circus is currently below us in the big pen. I don't know how she got here or why or anything other than I'm sure it's Heidi."

Fink, poor guy, looked a little shell-shocked, but Ellie had come over and put her arm around him.

"Did you just say there was an elephant below us?" she asked.

"Yes."

"Oh, wow. The boys are going to love this."

"We'd better not tell them tonight," Fink said quickly, looking around, presumably for his rambunctious off spring.

"You're probably right. As always, dear," Ellie said, with a bit of a glint in her eye.

Jillian suspected Ellie wouldn't tell the boys, but she'd be below the barn herself, checking out the elephant.

Jillian had opened her mouth to offer to take Ellie down. Heidi was sweet and calm, but she was upset over her move and more than likely missing her sister. She probably wouldn't get violent, but Jillian would feel horrible if she did.

But Fink beat her to speech. "I can see what you're thinking, and no. Absolutely not."

Ellie's eyes widened. "What?" She tilted her head. Ellie had definitely perfected the totally innocent look.

"You want to go see the elephant," Fink stated with a glower.

Ellie blinked. "Oh, Honey. What a great idea! I'd just love to." She moved closer and smiled sweetly up into Fink's face. "You'll come with me, right?"

"I'll take you both down, if you want," Jillian offered.

"Let's wait until after we have this cleaned up and the boys are in bed," Fink suggested, obviously no match for his wife's feminine wiles.

"Okay, honey." Ellie grinned, and Fink put a hand up and cupped her cheek for a moment.

Jillian started to move off, but Fink's voice stopped her. "Don't you need a permit or something for that?"

"Yes. I do. I'll have to look into getting something tomorrow." She chomped on the gum that McKoy had given her. "Is it okay for us to keep her? At least until I can figure something out?" She'd love to keep her for real, but she wasn't under any delusions that she'd be able to afford it. Plus, surely Heidi would want to be somewhere other than stuffed under someone's barn.

"As long as we're not breaking any laws, that's fine." He gave McKoy a look.

"I'll actually have to look the particulars up. I don't deal with elephants very often." McKoy shrugged.

Fink and Ellie smiled. "You do that and let us know. In the meantime, I'm sure Jillian will know how to take care of her. Is it going to be too cold for her tonight?"

Jillian chomped harder. "I don't know."

"Well, if we need to, she can go down to the training room in the dog kennel. There's plenty of room there, you'll just have to clean it up in the morning."

"Thanks," Jillian said. She hadn't thought of that. They'd converted an old shed into dog kennels, with kennels and dog doors all around the outside. On the inside area of the building, there was a big room that she used for the dog obedience classes that she'd just started a few months ago. The floor was cement with a big drain in the middle. It would be easy to clean and disinfect. That's what they'd designed it for.

She looked over to see McKoy studying her. His dark blue gaze made her want to squirm, but she didn't allow herself that luxury. She'd hoped to hide things from him. Knew she'd still have to. And he wasn't the kind of man who would let things slide. He'd play by the rule book. Unfortunately, she might not be able to do that.

She needed him on her side. She touched her tongue to her lip and gave him her coyest smile.

He blinked. Exactly the reaction she was going for. Now she needed to see his cow eyes.

Except, instead of his eyes glazing over, and his brain going on hiatus, his eyes narrowed. His lips pressed together.

She yanked her eyes away. Typical government employee. If she had the money she could bribe him. Otherwise she'd be on his hit list.

She grew up skirting the edges of Mexican law. She could handle one little dog catcher in Pennsylvania.

The next morning, McKoy walked into the kitchen wearing a pair of gym shorts. The sky was just starting to lighten with the promise of the sunrise.

Uncle Roy already had the coffee brewing. He sat at the table with the morning paper, his glasses perched on his nose, and his dogs, two scruffy mixed breeds, whining at his feet.

"'Morning, old man," McKoy said as he grabbed his coffee mug from the cupboard.

"'Morning, whippersnapper," Uncle Roy said without looking up from the paper. It was their standard greeting every morning he was home.

He poured a cup of coffee. He drank it black.

He shuffled to the door. "I'm taking your dogs out."

"Wait," Uncle Roy barked.

McKoy froze with his hand on the door knob. "Yeah?" Usually Uncle Roy barely communicated until he'd had two cups of coffee and read the paper, every word, including the comics—especially the comics—from front to back.

"Twisty said to make them sit before you let them out."

"Oh?" McKoy said. Twisty was some old neighbor lady who checked on Uncle Roy when McKoy was out of town. Sometimes she even came on days when he was working in the area. Apparently she was a drill sergeant with dogs. He wouldn't know, since he'd never met her.

"Yeah," Uncle Roy said. "Sit," he barked out.

McKoy hid a smile. Uncle Roy wouldn't speak softly when a shout would do.

But to McKoy's surprise, both mutts put their butts on the floor. Maybe Twisty knew what she was doing. He'd like to meet her, and he'd told Uncle Roy as much, but some people were put off by his job, and he figured that maybe she was one of those.

"Now you reward them by letting them out," Uncle Roy said as he rubbed his mustache.

McKoy opened the back door. "Okay, guys." That's all it took and the dogs leaped up, bounding out into the large, fenced yard.

Standing on the porch, leaning against the post, McKoy watched the sky explode in color and slowly fade as the sun peeked over the mountain.

By the time he made it back in, Uncle Roy was just folding up the paper.

"I picked some of these up yesterday when I was out." McKoy put a couple of over fifty-five living brochures on the table.

Uncle Roy looked at them, then shook his head. "Not interested. None of 'em will let me take my dogs."

"It's up to you, but if I don't get this promotion at work, my traveling schedule is not going to slow down. If anything, I might end up getting transferred, which could be even worse. I'd only be able to come home on the weekends I'm not on call."

"Don't go borrowing trouble. There's no reason for you not to get the promotion."

"I'm not the only one qualified." And he definitely wasn't the one pursuing the promotion the most aggressively. "It's not a given."

"I know. But I'm not gonna think like that. I want to stay here, so I'm just going to plan on it." Uncle Roy fixed his lips in that stubborn set that McKoy easily recognized. Anytime he'd ever needed corrected during his growing-up years, that's the lip set he'd see.

"Plus," Uncle Roy said, crossing his arms over his chest and leaning back in his chair. "Twisty will take care of me. I already told her she could move in."

McKoy blinked. He'd bought the house from Uncle Roy several years ago. He didn't get too bent out of shape when Uncle Roy wanted things done a certain way, acting like he still owned the house. McKoy didn't really care whether the daffodils they planted were white or yellow, or, to be honest, whether they even planted daffodils.

But inviting someone to move in?

"I thought she lived in the neighborhood?" Their house stood on the outskirts of Love. He'd assumed that Twisty, whoever she was, lived in town or somewhere close.

"She does. And she has a job where she lives, but I know if I need her to move, she'd bunk in our spare room. She's not picky."

McKoy snorted. A woman who wasn't picky? Now that he needed to see to believe. He'd bet Twisty would have an opinion on the color of the daffodils. She'd want the toilet paper hung a certain way, too. He'd have to finally fix that leaky faucet. His sisters had never been satisfied and always looked out for the next new thing. His mom, too, apparently, since she left his dad for someone new and exotic. His fiancée had found someone more exciting, too.

If he wasn't careful, he could end up getting kicked out of his own home.

Chapter 4

J illian put her head down on her small, apartment-sized table. First thing Monday morning, she'd tried to see about the permit, and she'd been right. In order to apply for a permit, a person had to be a United States citizen.

She had plenty of experience with elephants, which was another requirement, but she didn't really have anyone who would be a witness to it. She supposed she could get ahold of her cousins in Mexico, but since the circus had been put out of business, they'd lost touch. Still, family was family, at least in Mexico. In America, not so much. But she couldn't complain, because her claim to being related to Ellie's deceased husband's family was dubious at best, and relied heavily on word-of-mouth, since his name never made it onto her birth certificate.

She pushed the papers aside and grabbed her cell phone. Carlos was in her contacts. She pulled him up and left a message about needing fake papers for her elephant. Hopefully he'd be able to do his job and figure out exactly what she needed.

She'd fed her dogs and Heidi. She had some time before her first private obedience lesson, so she grabbed her headphones and headed out for a jog.

There wasn't much happening at the Christmas tree office this time of year, and there were no cars there. It wasn't far from Fink and Ellie's house, where Ellie was probably dreaming up decorations for this fall while Fink and their three boys were in school.

The drive was gravel and her feet crunched into the stones until she hit the blacktop road and kicked her speed up a notch.

It was early—not quite eight—and the cool spring air felt re-freshing on her face. Her problems with Heidi, with owing the coyote who'd helped her across the border, with owing for her ride from Arizona, not getting a permit, and McKoy's impending visit all wanted to run in a loop around her head. But she shoved them aside. Her jog was about relieving her worries not reliving them.

She searched for something pleasant to think about. McKoy's blue eyes came into her mind. The short, blond hair. The broad shoulders. How he'd helped her instead of giving her a hard time. The way his eyes had darkened when she danced in his arms.

Maybe she'd better think of something else. They weren't friends, and were quite likely to end up enemies before everything was said and done.

Mrs. Stewart, who lived in the first house on the outskirts of Love, was out on her porch in her pink house coat. Jillian waved as she jogged by. Mrs. Stewart called out a greeting.

The neighbors tolerated Jillian, but like many small towns, were distrustful of strangers. Rightfully so in some cases. Jillian had heard some of them talking about her not being "quite right."

She supposed that anyone who'd grown up in the circus would not be "quite right." Maybe the circus would still be performing, but they couldn't afford the bribes the government workers were charging. There were also issues with drugs, although Jillian had stayed far away from that. Bribes and drugs were both big prob-lems in Mexico.

Here in America it was papers. Papers for her, papers for Heidi, papers to do pretty much anything.

If she had to choose between bribes and drugs, or papers, she supposed the papers were the lesser evil. Not by much.

Uncle Roy had Chatty and Bubbles on leashes, and from the look of it was attempting to practice the obedience lessons she'd been giving him.

She slowed to a walk. Chatty had wrapped her leash around his legs while Bubbles jumped up on Uncle Roy's knees.

Normally she didn't jog on Mondays, since she had obedience clients in the morning, so Uncle Roy's mouth dropped when he looked up and saw her.

"Twisty!" he called. "Gotta help me, girl. These beasts are getting the best of me."

"I'm coming, Uncle Roy." She opened the gate on the white picket fence and slipped through. With the fence and the big, branchy maple in the front yard, the wide, comfortable-looking front porch and fenced back yard, Uncle Roy had the house of her little girl dreams.

Her big girl dreams consisted of a house that was paid for. She didn't give a flip what it looked like. Although the white with green shutters would have been her favorite.

"Dogs are pack animals, Uncle Roy. You have to be clear about who is in charge."

"I was trying until this confoundit thing wrapped his leash around my legs."

Chatty was a girl, but she didn't bother to correct him.

She put her hands on her hips as she approached, then took one hand and lifted it like it was pressing down.

Both dogs laid their ears down and sat.

Jillian reached around his leg and untangled the leash, petting Chatty on her little white head while she did so.

"It's a miracle every time you do that."

His words made Jillian's lips quirk up. Uncle Roy was real. There was no pretense in him. Sure, he was a little louder than a person had to be, but he spoke his mind, which could sometimes be a bad thing, except Uncle Roy almost always had good things spinning in his brain.

"They just need to know you're the pack leader."

"I think you won that election."

"Then you're my vice-leader."

"I showed my nephew the trick you taught me."

Jillian fingered the leash in her hand. "Which trick?"

"The one where I make them sit before he takes them out."

"Oh, yeah? Was he impressed?"

"Sure was. I told him you were going to move in."

Jillian couldn't imagine that went over well, although she wasn't sure what kind of man lived with his uncle at his age. He was out of school and worked a job with unusual hours, so she figured he had to be at least twenty-three or twenty-four.

"I can't move in, Uncle Roy. I have my dogs to take care of." And now an elephant, too.

"I told you, you can use my car."

Jillian had been teaching Chatty to weave in and out between her hands and feet as she did slow cartwheels. She practiced it now.

"Your nephew will think I'm taking advantage of you."

"He wants to put me in a home."

Jillian happened to be upside down on her hands. Her look probably wasn't as effective that way. "Your nephew seems like he spoils you."

"I'm telling you, he's gone a lot and he wants me in a home. And I can't take my dogs to any of those places. Not to mention they stink."

"Can't argue with that," Jillian muttered, back on her feet. Chatty was doing great. She wasn't sure what kind of mixed breeds the dogs were, but they were both fairly easy to train. They were the right size, and would have made excellent circus performers.

But that part of her life was over.

So why was she teaching Chatty tricks?

"Do the handstand one," Uncle Roy said.

"You might have to help still," she said before she bent over in a handstand.

From that angle, the house looked huge. Bending her legs and back, she stretched until one foot was almost to the ground. "Hop on, Chatty," she said.

Chatty was the better behaved of the two, usually, and she stepped up on Jillian's ankle. Jillian slowly straightened her leg, and

Chatty adjusted her position until Jillian's leg was straight up and Chatty was perched on the bottom of her sneaker.

Jillian lowered her other leg the same way and Bubbles actually climbed on herself. A few seconds later Jillian was on her hands with both dogs perched on the bottoms of her Sneakers.

"They did it," the old man shouted. "Without any help." He did a fist pump.

She'd turned her head slightly to give Uncle Roy an upside-down smile when movement caught her eye and she straightened her head.

Blond with a square jaw. She didn't have any trouble recognizing the man who stepped out on the porch. But her brain didn't want to accept it.

Of course the next time she saw McKoy Rodning would be when she was upside down with two dogs perched on her feet. Lovely.

"Coming down," she said. They had some other things they did occasionally, but she was done with tricks. Something about the serious look on his face, or maybe it was the olive-green uniform that broadened his shoulders and emphasized his muscular legs, or the black boots that were braced apart on the porch. Or the way he had his hands crossed over his chest. Whatever it was, it gave Jillian the idea that he wasn't amused. The audience was not getting their money's worth.

And she was wrong about the age of Uncle Roy's nephew. McKoy must be almost thirty.

His look had made her a little weak in the elbows, but she managed to get her feet on the ground and straighten up without dumping the dogs or herself on the grass.

She cleared her throat, not sure what to say.

"Let me guess, Uncle Roy. This is Twisty." His voice was low. Maybe a little annoyed.

"Sure is. I didn't know you were watching." Uncle Roy turned to McKoy with a big grin. "She sure is something, isn't she?"

Jillian frantically tried to remember what all she'd told Uncle Roy. Hopefully he didn't decide to spill her life story. Had she told him she was in a circus in Mexico? She didn't want McKoy to start wondering if she were a legal citizen.

"I have a class, soon. Gotta run." She threw a quick wave at Uncle Roy.

"Hey, wait. I want to introduce you to my nephew."

"We've met." McKoy's voice was flat.

"We were in the wedding together on Saturday." Jillian felt she had to explain. She wasn't sure what that hooded look of McKoy's meant.

"I should have gone. But I didn't want to miss bingo." Uncle Roy patted Chatty's head.

McKoy crossed his arms over his chest. "You mean you didn't want to miss Bertha Wyndott's lemon cookies."

"Those, too." Uncle Roy winked at Jillian.

She had to smile. The man was sweet. And he loved his dogs. That showed a lot about a person's character, in her opinion.

"Well, I'd better be getting on."

"Take care," Uncle Roy called.

Jillian couldn't help but notice that McKoy didn't call anything out as she left. It was almost like he was angry with her. But she didn't do anything.

They'd not really spoken Saturday night as they'd helped clean up. So nothing had changed.

Unless he'd somehow discovered the truth about her.

But he couldn't have. It wasn't like her name was in his computer with a big black X beside it, alerting everyone that she didn't belong here.

She jogged along the sidewalk of Love until she came to the post office. Taking a small breather, she walked back and forth along the steps until she could head in without panting.

"Jillian Powell. I figured you'd be in this morning." Love's post-mistress, Janey Davis, bustled behind the counter. She had a pen stuck in her hair and her glasses on a chain around her neck.

"Mmm." Jillian nodded. "It's a nice morning."

"It's about time we get some decent weather around here. It's been winter for about five years, or seems like it anyways," Janey said. "My fingers are getting itchy to get to digging in the ground."

"Yeah." Jillian didn't have that affliction, but she didn't want to get into a moral argument about the superiority of people who worked the ground versus people who didn't, so she kept her expression bland.

"I heard tell there were some strange noises coming from the barn basement on Saturday." Janey had put her glasses on her face as she flipped letters in her hand, and now she peered over them. "Some folks in here are already this morning saying that old barn is haunted." Her voice lowered and she said "haunted" with a special shiver in her voice.

Janey fixed a level stare on Jillian.

Jillian pulled her show face. The one she used when someone else was performing. "Oh? I hadn't heard anything."

Janey pursed her lips and waited another few seconds before looking back down and continuing to sort the mail. "But I did hear the wedding was nice."

"It was. Beautiful. And Avery and Gator are so happy."

Jillian was happy for them, too. Maybe a small part of her longed to have what they had.

McKoy's face popped into her head.

Not with him! He could barely stand to look at her. There was no way she would have a happily ever after with him. Not to mention, since he was such a play-by-the-book kind of man, he wouldn't want to have anything to do with her anyway, other than making sure she was taking proper care of Heidi and that she had all the right confounded permits and papers.

Ugh.

"I heard they fixed that old barn up pretty nice." Janey had their bundle of mail, but she didn't act like she was planning on handing it over anytime soon.

"It was beautiful," Jillian said.

"You're putting on a show for Wildlife Days in town, so I hear."

"Yes. Mr. Peachy suggested I sign up to give a demonstration on dog obedience training. And Uncle Roy offered to let me use his dogs." Could she snatch the packet of mail without offending Janey? Probably not. Her fingers twitched, but she held them firmly on the counter.

"If you can train those rangy mongrels, you can train anything," Janey said with a shake of her head.

"They're coming along really well. They should do a great job next Saturday."

"I'll believe it when I see it. 'Twill be good for your business if it's true."

Jillian gave her a friendly smile. If she were going to grow her obedience business, she needed to court potential customers. "My demonstration is at one in the afternoon on the library lawn. Make sure you come see it."

"So..." Janey tapped the mail on the counter. "My daughter-in-law has a golden retriever that won't get house broke. She piddles on the kitchen floor every night. You handle things like that in your dog training business? Or do you just do tricks?"

Jillian's lips pressed together, but she didn't let the annoyed words out of her mouth. She waited until she could smile pleasantly. "I absolutely can help her housetrain her dog."

"I'll tell her."

"Sure. Tell her to give me a call and we'll set something up." Jillian couldn't help the happy little thrill that skipped down her backbone. If she could get Janey's daughter's dog trained and make them happy, Janey would be about the best advertising she could hope for. Pretty much everyone in town stopped at the post office.

That could really help her business.

When she'd come over from Mexico, she'd planned on a house-keeping job, but that fell through. But things were working out well. Fink and Ellie had taken her under their wing, and had treated her better than she'd ever expected. Of course, she'd helped them when they were having a hard time, as well. Still, she needed to send money to the coyote. Most of them were involved in drugs, and she didn't want to get on their hit list.

Janey finally handed over her mail. Jillian jogged down the steps and headed down the road that would loop her back to the farm, with two main things on her mind—expanding her dog training business so she could get the coyote paid, and getting something figured out about Heidi and keeping McKoy satisfied until she did.

Chapter 5

T uesday afternoon McKoy made his first unscheduled visit to the farm. He stopped at the old farmhouse first, just because it seemed polite to let Fink and Ellie know that he was there. He didn't think they had much to do with the elephant. They certainly didn't have previous experience with it.

He parked next to the porch and got out. He'd deliberately waited until school would be out, so Fink would be home.

Fink and Ellie's three boys were playing in the yard. The called out a greeting and yelled, "Mom and Dad are in the house," as they chased each other around, a rangy looking dog nipping and following at their heels.

McKoy couldn't remember their names, but he yelled a "thanks" and took the porch steps two at a time.

Fink opened the door just as McKoy lifted his hand to knock. "Come on in. You're just in time to join us for our afternoon snack. Ellie always has something good ready when we get home."

McKoy opened the screen door and leaned against the door frame. "Thanks. It smells good, but I just wanted to stop in and let you know I need to make an inspection on the elephant."

Fink's brows knitted. "Is there something wrong?"

"Not really. But until she has a permit, I can't just let it slide. So she agreed to two inspections per week, one planned, one surprise. The planned ones will be on Saturdays. This is the surprise."

"Oh, I see." Fink shrugged.

"I didn't want to go down to the barn without telling you."

"Of course not. But Jillian is really the one who is responsible for it."

"I know."

Ellie walked over, a dishtowel in her hand. "She's at the dog kennel just finishing up a group lesson. She'd probably like to accompany you. The elephant seemed very nice, but it obviously knew Jillian."

"Hmm." McKoy had hoped that Jillian would go. His experience with elephants was limited to Gator's wedding.

If McKoy ever got married, which was unlikely to happen, he hoped that the most memorable thing at his wedding was not an elephant.

"I have to agree with Ellie," Fink said, with a loving smile at his wife. "You better take Jillian along."

"I'll stop at the kennel and see if she'll go. If it's okay, I'll leave my truck here."

"Sure." Fink nodded. "You don't have to ask. If the inspection is your job, just do it. You can probably get Jillian's number to let her know when you're here, or whatever."

"Does she stay here?"

"She's got her stuff down at the little house where Harper lived before she moved to Chile." Fink nodded in the direction of what McKoy would call the mother-in-law bungalow.

"Oh." He'd thought she'd lived in the house with Fink and Ellie. It didn't matter. He wasn't going to her house.

"Thanks. I appreciate your hospitality." Some people were downright ignorant to him. Like he was inspecting their property just to make life hard for them. He appreciated the people who treated him like a fellow human just doing his job.

"No problem," Fink said, his scholarly face smiling. "If Jillian can't go down with you, and you want someone to go along, let me know. I don't mind being your backup."

McKoy smiled and waved as he backed out of the door and let it close behind him.

The dog kennel was down past the barn. McKoy had to walk past the tiny house that Jillian lived in. He gave it a few curious glances. What kind of woman worked in a circus, trained dogs, helped old men out, and kept an elephant on the side?

If he was looking for eccentric, which he wasn't, Jillian definitely fit that bill.

But he couldn't think about her like that. Yeah, there was a magnetism in her dancing, black eyes that pulled at something deep inside of him. However, not only was she trouble, but a woman like her would definitely agree with his former fiancée—McKoy was boring.

He didn't need Jillian to say it for him to know it was true.

The area around her house was tidy. A small rocking chair took up most of the room on the covered stoop. Lace curtains hung in all the windows. More curious than he wanted to admit to being, McKoy kept walking and didn't try to see in the widows. He had a feeling someone like Jillian might be messy.

He didn't necessarily need things neat, but he liked order and schedules. Something else that would probably clash with Jillian's personality.

There were six or eight cars parked along the back side of the kennel as he walked around the corner. Five or six dogs ran in and out their individual dog doors, barking and jumping. From the outside, the place looked clean, the dogs healthy.

Carefully he opened the door, not wanting to interrupt her class.

But the door opened into an entry way. The next door had a big glass window and he could see Jillian in the middle of the floor, her back to him, while eight people with their dogs on leashes, sitting at their sides, faced Jillian, listening intently as she said something about homework for next week.

After a sentence or two, she dismissed the class. McKoy didn't want to give the impression that the "dog catcher" had it out for Jillian—might not be good for her business—so he leaned against the wall and tried to keep a pleasant look on his face as people filed out.

Some of them knew him, others recognized his uniform, and everyone said "hi" at least.

Jillian walked out with the last student, a Great Dane who pulled on his small, female mistress. McKoy got the impression that the dog was the head of that relationship.

Jillian was deep in conversation and didn't look his way. "He has to know you're in charge."

"But he's so strong, I'm really not in charge."

Jillian held out her hand for the leash. The woman gave it to her and Jillian commanded the dog to sit. It obeyed instantly.

"Now, when you start walking and he starts pulling, just pull this way, then that." She demonstrated over the Dane's head. "You don't want to hurt him, although he's a big boy, and he's strong. You don't want to choke him, either. But you want him to learn that pulling you is not pleasant."

She handed the leash back. "You work on that some for next week. If you come a little early, I can work with you and Spencer before the other students get here."

"Oh, thanks. I'd appreciate that."

When the woman turned around again, McKoy recognized Kristy Hammond. He'd been out at her place over a rabid skunk a year ago or so, but she was a lifelong resident of Love, same as him, and they were acquainted.

Her dog pulled her toward him, stopping and jumping. McKoy had been around enough dogs to have had a split second to see what the dog had planned. He sidestepped, and the dog pawed air before crashing back down to its feet.

"I'm sorry," Kristy said. "Good reflexes."

"It's okay. Seems like this is a good place to bring him if he needs some manners."

"He's a sweetheart, but he does need manners." She tilted her head. "I bought a trap because I have some raccoons messing around in my shed. If I catch one, will you relocate it for me?"

That wasn't necessarily on his list of job requirements, but he nodded. "Sure. Call me and I'll deal with it."

"I don't want to hurt it."

"I know. I'll set it free somewhere it'll be safe. From humans, anyway." Not that raccoons had that many wild predators.

"Thanks, McKoy." She lifted a foot and her dog dragged her out the door.

McKoy's lip twitched, but he didn't laugh. Wouldn't have been nice.

All of the other students and their owners had left.

"I suppose you're here to see Heidi."

"That's right." He hooked his thumbs in his pockets. Jillian didn't look thrilled to see him. In fact, her mouth was flattened down tight, and she looked put out. Which irritated him, some. He could have fined her on Saturday.

"I'll go down with you, just let me turn the lights out." She didn't look at him, and her flashing black eyes seemed more subdued today. He had the feeling yesterday she'd been a little embarrassed that he caught her upside down with his uncle's dogs on her feet. But she wasn't exactly acting embarrassed.

"You don't have to come. I can go myself." He'd brushed up on the law, and knew what he was looking for.

"You'll make her nervous. She's never hurt anyone. She's sweet and gentle, but I don't know what she's been through lately." Jillian flipped out the lights to the large, open room, and walked by him before he could open the outside door for her.

Every move she made was accentuated with a flowing grace that fascinated him. Even her walk was somehow effortlessly elegant. Sensuous.

He stumbled over the doorframe.

She looked back over her shoulder, a question on her face as she checked to see that he was okay.

"I'm fine. Not used to the jam that sticks up like that." He might as well have said he wasn't used to walking in his boots. No, the problem was that he couldn't take his eyes off her to be bothered to watch where he was going.

He needed to remember she wasn't interested in him that way, and it would be dangerous and dumb for him to allow his brain to keep going in that direction.

"Did you find the papers the elephant travelled with?" he asked.

"One minute." She walked back inside, coming out in less than a minute with a large envelope.

He took it from her hand and pulled the papers out. He'd done some checking since Saturday, and the papers in his hand seemed like they were correct.

Jillian stood in front of him, twisting her hands. She stopped when he looked up after studying the papers.

"These look good to me, although I should admit I've never seen elephant papers before."

She lifted a slender shoulder. "That's what I received."

"We'll call them good. Thanks." He put the papers back in the envelope and handed it to her. She disappeared back in the building and returned just as quickly as the last time.

The lot was empty as they walked through it and around the building. The dogs in the kennels still barked and paced. McKoy didn't try to hide the fact that he was checking out the kennels, which were as clean as any kennels he'd ever inspected.

"Do they meet with your approval?" Jillian asked, with a bit of defiance in her voice.

"You obviously do a good job." McKoy turned to her and spoke sincerely.

Her brows raised. She wasn't expecting his praise. Why would that be? The kennels were clean, and he wasn't afraid to say so.

"Thanks," she mumbled, her eyes going back in front of her.

"You know I'm not out here to get you," he said, because he felt like that's exactly what she thought.

She pulled her cheek in, chewing on it again.

McKoy reached for the pack of gum he always kept in his pocket. He'd had a tobacco habit when he was younger, and the gum was a help when the rogue urge to light up hit him. He held it out.

She glanced over, then her gaze shot up to his, her eyes wide.

"Peace offering," he said, hoping for a smile.

Her lips pressed together, one side twitching up.

"Or maybe I'm just trying to rescue the inside of your cheek, which you seem intent on eating."

Her teeth flashed and her black eyes sparkled. She tossed her head, but took a piece of his gum.

"No one has ever called me on it before, but you're right. I do have a tendency to chew on my cheek." She shrugged.

"We all have bad habits, I suppose." He'd never met anyone who didn't. Often a visit from him brought out the worst in people.

Her face might have smiled, but her shoulders had not relaxed. She still held him in suspicion. He didn't feel like their relationship was easy enough for him to ask why. For some reason, he wanted that right.

They reached the barn, and a rumbling sound greeted them.

"She hears us," Jillian murmured.

"I didn't know elephants made a sound like that."

"They'll chirp, too."

His face must have shown his disbelief, because she glanced at it and said, "Not like a bird. A little deeper and fuller, but still definitely a chirp."

"You've spent a lot of time with elephants." He'd gotten that impression on Saturday when she moved with such confidence and security around the large animal.

"Yes."

"And when I start asking about it, you become monosyllabic."

"I'm a private person."

She didn't say "and you're prying" but she didn't need to. The accusation hung between them. Well, there were questions he'd need to ask for his job, and she'd have to answer those. But she couldn't be more clear that the extent of their relationship would be him in an official capacity. If only his eyes didn't want to devour her every movement. And if only he didn't have a hundred questions on his tongue that had nothing to do with his job and everything to do with wanting to know more about her.

She led him around the barn and into the barnyard, where he could see that she'd been reinforcing the old, wooden fences with larger posts and beams.

He had known that the half-rotted-looking fences wouldn't pass an inspection.

"You've been doing the fencing yourself?" Posts, beams, and a spade, along with what looked like a solid steel digging bar that was older than he was and probably almost as heavy, lay against the stone barn foundation.

"Yes. One of the requirements is that I have a solid, secure area to keep her. This is much bigger than the required 1,500 square feet, but I wanted her to be able to be outside in the sun if she chooses."

That was quite a job for one slender woman.

"Did you tell Fink and Ellie that you were doing this?"

"In general terms. They are both busy, Fink with his job and Ellie with the kids and planning on the farm for this year. I know they'd help, but I couldn't ask. They've already done so much for me." Her voice got fainter and she looked away.

"I can't see in under the barn. I'm going to need to walk in." He was sure it was clean and that Heidi had feed and fresh water, but it was his job to check. He couldn't neglect it, although it was getting harder and harder to not want to treat Jillian like a job. Her determination to make that fence—one strong enough to stop an elephant—by herself, made him admire her. And want to help.

But that would be completely unethical—helping to build the fence he needed to inspect. It wasn't written in his contract that he couldn't help, exactly, but common sense dictated that it didn't make sense.

"When do you think you'll have the fence finished?" he asked as she opened the gate and led him through.

She shrugged and pushed a strand of hair back out of her face. "I've been working on it every chance I get around my clients and taking care of the dogs in the kennel."

Her hand started to fall back to her side. His brain didn't form the cohesive thought, but he reached out and grabbed her wrist, turning her palm up.

She tried to pull it back, but his fingers tightened. Broken, bloody blisters marred the entire inside of her hand.

His stomach cramped. It wasn't hard to imagine how badly they must be hurting her right now, nor the agony she'd be in when she started back to work on the fence. Just picking up that monstrosity of a digging iron would shoot pain clear to her shoulder.

Her long graceful fingers were red and inflamed. The soft skin that touched his hand was white and delicate. Some kind of strong emotion backed up in his chest. It came out in anger.

"Don't you believe in gloves?" he growled.

"I didn't have any?" She looked at him oddly, like she couldn't figure out why he'd be upset about her hands.

His teeth ground together. "There's a hardware store in town, less than two miles away. They have a shelf full."

"I wanted to get it done." Her feet were planted in a defiant posture.

"It would take ten minutes to drive there and pick up a pair."

"I can't drive."

McKoy froze. She didn't have a license? His brain started whirling over the possibilities. Maybe in the city a person could get away with no license, with all the public transportation available. But around here? There was no subway, no bus stops, a taxi would cost a day's pay, and Uber? He supposed that might be a possibility, but he doubted it.

She pulled, harder this time, and he let her hand slip out of his, the softness and warmth gliding over his callouses like skates on ice.

He dropped his hand and fisted it at his side.

"You can't drive? Or you don't have a car?"

"I don't have a car or a license." Her words seemed to be pulled out of her, and she had started to walk away, telling him the discussion was over.

He'd never met someone more stubborn or more determined to keep her secrets to herself.

He supposed he couldn't expect her to trust him.

Following her back, he squinted into the darkness as his eyes adjusted to the light. The elephant flapped her ears as Jillian murmured softly to her. The long gray trunk came out and tapped down Jillian's hand as she held it out.

Jillian walked closer and stroked the elephant's side.

McKoy came near enough to see the water and feed were clean and full. There were several big piles of dung on the floor, but they were all shiny and new-looking.

Jillian kept the place as clean as her kennels, and it was obvious she loved the elephant. Just as obvious was that the elephant loved her. McKoy couldn't blame it.

Chapter 6

Jillian's hands burned like the digging iron was red-hot. But she couldn't stop. McKoy had been very interested in the fence, and it was a requirement, permit or no permit.

Her fake papers had fooled him, although the guilt that she felt as he said they were good enough almost choked her. Carlos had done a great job, and she would make sure to tell him so, but it didn't make her feel any better about deceiving McKoy.

Yeah, he did seem like a person who played by the rules, but there was something very appealing about a man who lived by a moral code. She wished she were worthy of that kind of man, but in order to keep Heidi, she was afraid her lying had only begun.

She lifted the digging iron up, trying to ignore the pain that burned up her arms and traveled down, clear into the small of her back. Her entire body hurt, but she needed to get this fence done.

She slammed down with the digging iron into the hole she had. It was almost deep enough to set the post.

"Let me."

Shivers raced down her back at the sound of a familiar, deep voice. A big hand wrapped around the handle of the iron between her two. She stared at it before lifting her face and meeting those deep blue eyes. His expression was serious, and his body crowded hers. She let go and stepped back.

"These aren't going to take the pain away." He held up a brand-new pair of gloves. She blinked, part of her wanting to refuse, but after a few seconds, she took them.

He reached in his pocket. "But this might make it bearable."

A small tube of pain killers lay in his hand.

Her eyes went from the tube to his face and back again. His lip was turned back, like he hated giving her the pills, but he probably knew she wasn't going to stop.

She'd never thought of taking pain killers. They were for headaches, cramps, and maybe the flu.

"Thanks," she said, taking the small vial.

He pulled a bottle of water out of his pocket. He'd changed from his olive-green work uniform into jeans and an old black T-shirt that clung to his back and rippled as he moved.

The water was unopened. She took it and swallowed the pills with several large gulps.

"Sit down and give them a few minutes to kick in." He jerked his head over to where Heidi stood in the corner, watching. "Back when I was a kid, I spent a few summers baling hay and fixing fences. Back before the factory farms put the family dairy farms out of business. I have a little experience, anyway."

He'd begun working before he'd finished talking, and she backed away to give him room.

After a minute or so, he set the iron aside and used the spade, scooping the dirt he'd loosened and setting it aside.

"I assume you have permission from Fink and Ellie to put this up," he said as he pushed the shovel in the hole.

She tore her eyes away from the way his biceps flexed as he maneuvered the shovel. "Yes. Of course."

"Just didn't want them coming down here and getting all angry after seeing what we're doing."

"No. They won't. They've been better to me than I deserve. They both said whatever I needed to do to make the place so that Heidi could stay, I could." And they'd offered to spot her the money, or she wouldn't have the posts and bars she needed.

"That's good. From what I looked into, you need a fence strong enough that she can lean into it without being able to push it down."

"Yes. That's what I found too. That's why I have the iron bars and big posts."

"You shouldn't have been handling that stuff by yourself."

"You have no right to tell me what to do." She wanted to bite her tongue off. She didn't need to provoke him. "I assume you're here in your civilian capacity."

"Yeah." He had taken the digging iron back in hand and it thudded into the ground, his shoulder muscles bunching.

It occurred to her that this could be a conflict of interest to him.

He didn't seem like the kind of guy that would allow conflicts of interest.

She tore the tag off the gloves and gingerly put them on her hands. The pain had diminished to a dull thud, but they still hurt. Regardless, she walked over and grabbed the spade, ready to scoop the dirt and rocks out of the hole when McKoy quit pounding on it. She needed to have something to do other than stare at his back and the interesting way he filled out his jeans.

But McKoy didn't allow her to use it. Rather, when he was done with the iron, he set it on the ground and leaned it toward her.

"Trade me," he said.

"I'll do it," she argued, even though just lifting the shovel brought tears to her eyes.

"Your hands can't take it."

"You're not wearing gloves."

He took the shovel, giving her no choice but to grab the digging iron or let it fall. "I'll show you my hands when we're finished. I started working with them when I was a kid, and they've developed such a thick set of callouses, I could do this all day, and they'd be fine."

"Mine will be fine, too."

"I've had hands that look like yours, blistered and blood— Granted, it was years ago, but you don't forget pain like that

She couldn't deny they hurt.

"It's gonna be days or even a week or more before you can use them without pain." He lifted a brow at her as he dumped more dirt on the pile that had doubled since he'd started. "I'm here. I can help. Let me."

"I don't put up with people who try to tell me what to do." Again, her mouth got the best of her. Why couldn't she remember she needed this man to like her?

But one side of his mouth quirked up. "I figured that out already."

"Didn't seem to change your words."

"Nope. I don't typically put up with people who don't listen to me. Guess we're both treading new ground." He dumped the last shovel full of dirt on the ground and leaned the handle to her.

She took it, with a twinge in her hand and one near her heart at his solid jaw and the bit of humor in his eyes.

"I've never helped a person become compliant so I could inspect them. Not real sure it's legal, but I couldn't let this go." His voice rumbled like the far-away thunder of an approaching storm. Soft and low, but with potential power. She found herself attracted to the combination.

"Thank you," she said. Because as stubborn and determined as she was, it was obvious that she would never have been able to continue working on the fence.

"I think this hole's good." He looked around on the ground. "You have the next one planned out?"

She picked up the tape measure. "The bars are eight feet long. I've been making sure the posts are spaced that far apart."

She measured from the middle of the hole he just finished to the next.

They worked in silence for the next hour or so. In that time, McKoy was able to get the holes dug. The top of his shirt, front and back, was darker with sweat, and his forehead glistened, but he worked at a steady pace, and seemed to be able to keep it up indefinitely.

"There." He shoved the spade shovel in the ground and rested his foot on it. "Holes are dug."

"I would never have been able to get that done. I really appreciate your help."

He nodded at the bottle of water that she'd left over where they'd started.

"You want any more of that?" he asked.

She walked over and picked it up, carrying it over and handing it to him. "No. You go ahead."

"Thanks." He twisted the cap off and finished the bottle. Jillian stared at how his throat worked, how the cords of his neck stood out, how he stood, straight and true before her, tired and covered in sweat for no other reason than to help her.

Why?

He leaned the shovel against the stone wall of the barn foundation. "Give me a minute. I have some bags of ready-mix cement on the back of my truck. I'll back it down here and we can set those posts."

Her eyes widened. He wasn't done? She glanced at the sky. They had maybe another hour of daylight.

"We can use my headlights if we need to, although if we put a hurry on, we might get it done without them." He screwed the cap back on the bottle. "We'll need water to mix the cement." He handed her the bottle. "Maybe you could fill this up, too, if you don't mind."

"Of course." The least she could do was fill up his water bottle.

He strode off, and she hurried around to get the hose out and screw it on, wincing at the pain in her hands.

She took her gloves off to fill the bottle, and her blisters were oozing goo. Her hands had stiffened from the time of inactivity and now it was painful to even try to bend her fingers. She couldn't imagine how it would feel without the pain meds. How soon until she could take more?

She had just finished carefully pulling her gloves back on, the hose screwed onto the faucet and lying in a coil at her feet, when McKoy's pickup backed around the corner, the tail gate down and bags of ready-mix cement lying on the back with a wheelbarrow upside down over them.

Hurrying over, she opened the gate to the barnyard so he could back through. She closed it carefully behind him. As far as she knew, Heidi hadn't tried to push against the rickety fence, or really hadn't even come out from under the barn much, seeming to prefer the security of having walls around her over the open space of the barnyard. As used to being in an enclosed space as Heidi was, that made sense that she'd need some time to get used to the new surroundings, especially without her sister and constant companion to comfort her.

Still, Jillian didn't want to take the chance.

She walked over to McKoy's truck as he shut the motor off and climbed out, her heart slamming against her chest. How was she going to pay for this?

She'd used up every cent in her bank account to have the posts and bars delivered, and she owed Fink and Ellie for the material. She did have money in her business account from boarding fees and class fees, but she needed to buy dog food and pay Ellie and Fink rent. They weren't charging her, but she couldn't be a complete freeloader. Still, her personal "salary" that she'd budgeted for herself was completely spent until Friday.

"Can I wait until Friday to write you a check for this?" she asked, not figuring there was any point at beating around the bush.

"We can talk about it later," he said, grabbing the handles of the wheelbarrow and lifting it off of the back of his truck.

The ease with which he manhandled it threatened to derail her thoughts, but she tried to focus. "I've never priced out cement. I don't even have any idea of what it costs."

He stopped with his hand on the bag. "You didn't ask me to help. I came here and pushed my way in. I'd hardly ask for money for doing that. Now, what I wouldn't mind is if you stopped giving me those suspicious glares like I'm about ready to rip your grandmother's purse off her shoulder and run off with it every time you see me."

She put a hand on her hip, flinching a little from the pain. "Where I come from, government officials usually make decisions based on how much money a person has."

"That's not the way it happens here. Not with me."

"I've been figuring that out, but I can't just shove my experiences aside."

He dumped the opened bag of ready-mix concrete in the wheelbarrow, then looked up at her, grey dust coating his shirt and arms. "Where are you from? What city? Did you report the crooked officials?"

She shook her head, panic bubbling in her stomach. He couldn't find out she wasn't a citizen.

"I know it sometimes takes justice a while to work, but don't let that keep you from coming forward. Do you have proof?"

Why had she said anything?

"No. No proof."

His dark eyes narrowed and he stared at her. "If you work for the government, as I do, you're a servant of the people, and you should remember that. Because the 'government' represents the people." He used his fingers to do air quotes around "government."

She curled her toes, because it was too painful to move her hands, but she needed to fidget a little. Obviously the man practiced what he preached. He was here, wasn't he? She'd been judging him too harshly.

McKoy gave her another searching look, then shook his head. "Before I put the water in this, I want to run a string to make sure we get these posts level."

He went to the back door and rooted around, bringing back an orange string and a longish thing that Jillian thought might be a level.

He put her to work holding the string, then the level, until he was satisfied. "It's not going to be the straightest thing in the world, but it's going to look straight, anyway."

"It's going to be straighter than it would have been if I would have done it, since I wouldn't have gone to those lengths."

He grinned. "Did the lady just say she was happy I was helping?"

Jillian knew her mouth was open, but it took her a few seconds to find her voice. Was the straight-laced government employee flirting with her?

"Maybe." Possibly he could tell from her tone how uncertain she was.

The idea of flirting with him to try to get him to overlook her situation with Heidi, or at the very least her citizenship situation, had crossed her mind. But he hadn't struck her as the type of man who would break rules, even for his own family.

That wasn't the only reason she hadn't tried, though. Because it didn't sit right with her, either. She didn't want to be that kind of person, even though she'd seen it work for others. She supposed she'd rather be deported than be a deceiver.

He didn't say anything more, but turned and grabbed the hose, squirting water in the wheelbarrow on top of the dry ready-mix cement.

"Don't you have to measure that?" she asked when he quit squirting.

His broad shoulder lifted. "I guess you're supposed to. It's just kind of common sense, though."

Jillian wasn't sure she saw the "common sense" aspect, but she didn't say anything. He showed her how to set the post, then had her hold it while he poured the cement around the base.

It was full dark. McKoy had turned his truck around and they were using the headlights by the time they set the last post. If she had to, she could mix the cement by herself, using "common sense" to estimate the amount of water. Which made her smile. It wasn't a skill she ever thought to have.

"What's so funny?" McKoy asked as he wheeled the wheelbarrow back from rinsing it out.

"Nothing, really. We don't have a fence, but we're closer than we were."

McKoy glanced down the line of posts before lifting the wheel barrow and putting it upside down on the back of his pickup. "Yep."

He slammed the tail gate shut. "I'm not going to be home tomorrow night. If you can wait until Friday, I'll give you a hand with the metal rails."

He was offering to come back? She could hardly believe it. Part of her wanted to jump on his offer. Another part warned her that he wasn't her friend. At least not when it came to the things she was hiding.

Playing it safe was never something she did well. "Okay. I'll feed you Friday, so don't worry about food."

He leaned a shoulder against his pickup and crossed his arms over his chest. "Not gonna turn down food."

"I'll be here when you get here." She could hardly believe she'd just made an appointment to see the dog catcher again. "I really appreciate your help. Thanks."

She gave him a smile.

He blinked and didn't move.

They stood behind the headlights, so she couldn't really read his expression. Maybe he didn't feel the little thrill that she did when their eyes met.

One corner of his mouth kicked up and he pushed off his truck. "See you Friday."

She jerked her head and walked ahead to open the gate. Holding it while he pulled through, she waved as he left, unsure if he returned the gesture.

She pushed the gate shut, leaning against it and sighing. Was she so pathetic that all it took to make her swoony over a guy was for him to lend a little muscle to her project?

A scream balled in her throat when she felt something touching her neck. Then she remembered Heidi.

"Hey, honey." She stroked the long, rough trunk. "Were you being shy tonight?"

The trunk touched through her hair, lifting it, then blowing. She laughed, still thinking about McKoy and why he might have helped her. Just to be nice? Maybe because she'd been checking on his uncle and training his dogs?

She turned to Heidi, pulling her phone out of her pocket to use the flashlight app. For the first time, she noticed that Heidi's ears were droopy and her head hung down some.

"What's the matter?" she asked. Like the elephant could tell her.

If she had to guess, she'd say that Heidi was missing her sister. She hadn't been able to get ahold of David, her cousin who owned the zoo in Mexico, and she'd have to give him another call when she got in. First, she needed to feed and water her elephant.

Chapter 7

T he next morning, McKoy went into the office before leaving for northern Pennsylvania. He bypassed his own office, there was nothing in there for him except paperwork and he barely ever used it. He walked directly to his supervisor's door, nodding at Loretta the receptionist as he passed.

He'd been thinking he should mention the elephant, but he knew once he did, his supervisor, Louie, would be after him to put pressure on Jillian to have a permit. She had thirty days. He could give her that without a struggle.

"Todd's in there with Louie," Loretta said.

"Thanks for letting me know." Todd was his main competition for the promotion. "Louie said to come straight to his office when I got in."

"Then go in," Loretta said, her hand moving back away from the intercom button.

McKoy tapped on the door before he opened it, years of courtesy drummed into him from his childhood.

"Come in," Louie called as McKoy pushed the door open.

The office was sparsely furnished. Louie sat behind the large, messy desk, and Todd sprawled in a chair opposite him. He looked up with a smirk when McKoy came in. As far as McKoy knew, they got along okay, although Todd maybe cut corners that McKoy wouldn't. He was also much better at buttering up the boss.

McKoy was much more serious about his job, and took all the extra work he could.

Todd liked to kick back on the evenings and weekends.

"Hey, great to see you." Louie nodded to the other chair. "You ready to head up north and set a trap for that bear that keeps getting into Elk County dumpsters?"

"I'm leaving after I get done here."

"Great." Louie stroked his beard. "Todd told me that he had a report of an elephant at the wedding just down the road from your house last weekend."

McKoy's heart fell. He'd thought they had gotten off without anyone noticing. He didn't want Todd getting the job. "Yeah, I'm on it."

Louie's brows narrowed. "Was there or was there not an elephant?"

"There is."

"Where's the permit?"

"She has thirty days, and I've already told her that."

"You make a report about it?"

McKoy's lips flattened. "Not yet."

Todd smirked. "She must be cute."

McKoy's jaw hardened, but he tried not to react. It's what Todd wanted. Todd knew he was straight as an arrow.

"Better write that report before you leave. Elephants are a little different than a dog that doesn't have a license."

"I know. I've already looked into the law, and I'm helping her comply." More than helping her, he was building her fence. That was probably crossing the line he'd spent his life trying not to cross, and he wasn't going to mention it in front of Todd, if he mentioned it at all. He probably would have helped any one of his neighbors build a fence. Thing was, he wasn't expecting to enjoy it.

He'd found out last night that along with the odd attraction he felt toward Jillian, he actually liked her. She'd worked alongside of him and had pretended the whole time that her hands weren't killing her when he knew doggone well that they had to hurt like heck. How could he not admire grit like that?

Then that little smile she'd given him before she left. A man could take a smile like that every day of his life.

Louie's hand dropped down from his beard. "I need a permit. You're right. She has thirty days. In the meantime, I want you out there every week."

"I'm on it. Actually going twice a week. One scheduled inspection, one unscheduled. Just did an unscheduled yesterday, and everything looked fine." Except for the fence, which was still going up.

Louie's eyes sparkled, and his beard parted as he smiled. "Figures you'd do double duty."

"Maybe I need to go inspect the elephant," Todd said, a speculative look on his face.

McKoy was walking a fine line. If he was too defensive, Todd would be suspicious, but he didn't want Todd hanging around Jillian. He didn't stop to question why.

He shrugged. "Up to Louie. If you want to take it from me, go ahead. But it's a mile from my house."

"But you're not going to be home tonight. Maybe the little elephant handler needs some help putting her big animal to bed." Todd didn't smile, but he lifted a suggestive eyebrow.

McKoy looked at Louie, who was shaking his head. "No. If McKoy has this under control, we're good. You take care of your assignments, Todd."

He stacked some papers on his desk and moved a folder. "You two know you are the only ones in the running for my position when I move up to regional. They'll be announcing which of you are taking my place, soon." He stroked his beard again. "I'm not sure when."

McKoy shrugged, although part of him was eager to know. If he got Louie's position, he wouldn't have to leave Uncle Roy alone at nights.

Louie looked at McKoy. "Elephant report. On my desk." His gaze moved to Todd. "Get to work."

McKoy walked out, Todd on his heels. As soon as the office door was shut, Todd said, "Is she cute? She must be young? Married?"

"Didn't ask." McKoy walked into his office. It was smaller but just as sparsely furnished as Louie's. Todd followed him in.

"Why does she have an elephant?"

McKoy walked around and sat at his desk, switching his computer on. "Someone gave it to her, I think."

"You think?"

"Technically she doesn't have to answer my questions."

"Maybe I need to go out. Women enjoy talking to me."

Not Jillian.

Where did that thought come from? McKoy had no idea who Jillian would talk to, although she seemed to loosen up to him after he'd been there for a while.

And she was going to cook for him Friday night.

Because he was building her fence.

He pictured her snapping black eyes and her sweet smile. Yeah, he was probably too boring for the likes of her, but he could enjoy Friday night. Even if he did have to build a fence first. He pulled up his computer program and started the report, eager for Friday.

Jillian paced in her kitchen. Her second Friday class had left an hour ago, and she almost had supper put together, but she was unsure what time McKoy was coming. She hadn't asked and didn't have his number. Five? Six? Four?

The wall clock said three thirty.

Rather than stressing, she figured she could try her distant cousin, Augusto, the person loosely in charge of the animals in the circus, for the hundredth time. He'd not returned any of her calls.

But if anyone knew why Heidi had been dropped off on her door step, it would be Augusto.

He answered after the second ring. "*Bueno.*"

After having been around her American family so long, the customary Mexican greeting felt off. "Augusto. It's Jillian."

"Jillian. My little darling. How are you doing?"

He wasn't interested in hearing about her sore hands. They didn't hurt as sharply as they had the night McKoy was here, but even holding her phone produced pinches of pain.

"I'm fine. Except I have an elephant in my barn."

"Are you working in the circus?" His voice was smooth and held no hint of surprise.

She leaned her head against the cold glass of the door window. "No. It closed. I know you know that. You were there."

"But a new circus, no? You are working in a new circus?"

She looked out at the dog kennel. "No! I'm done with the circus. I'm training dogs."

"What about your hair routine? Bending into shapes?"

"It's over, Augusto."

"Then you don't need Heidi?"

Jillian almost rolled her eyes, pretty sure that Augusto knew she wasn't in a circus of any kind and didn't need an elephant. "Where's Hazel?"

"I think someone bought her. I will have to check with David."

She hadn't been able to get ahold of David. "What am I supposed to do with Heidi?"

"She is in the US and none of us can get her permit."

"I'm not any different than any of you. I can't get her a permit, either." Jillian wrapped one arm around her stomach. Augusto wasn't any help at all.

"You have American father. You can do it."

"I don't even know my father's name. I'm not an American."

Augusto sighed. "We cannot take Heidi back to Mexico. We couldn't take her over the border. You need to keep her."

"Will you find out who bought Hazel?" Maybe the person would want a second elephant. Although why they wouldn't have bought two in the first place was too logical of a question.

A headache throbbed behind Jillian's eyes.

"I will try."

"Call me when you get it, please. I can't get a permit. Not to mention I need to find someone who can afford to feed her." McKoy's truck pulled down past the old farmhouse. It slowed as he approached the bend for the barn, but then he came straight, heading toward her small house.

"I will check," Augusto said.

"Thanks."

They hung up. In a few seconds, McKoy's boots thumped on the porch.

She ran a hand down her smooth hair, reminding herself this wasn't a date or even close, and didn't wait for him to knock, but opened the door before he had his hand raised.

"Hey," he said. His scent drifted to her, warm and male and intriguing. He had changed out of his uniform and wore a white T-shirt with clean but worn blue jeans and boots. His cheeks were smooth, like he'd shaved before he'd come, and his square jaw and deep blue eyes made her heart race.

She fought the urge to fidget. "Come on in."

He stayed on the porch. "Will it hold? We could probably have the fence done before dark."

Okay. That wasn't exactly romantic. She was getting all bothered by his scent and his eyes and those biceps, and he was worried about the fence. Exactly what he'd come for. She felt like a dope. "Sure. It's in the slow cooker. Let me turn it down. You can still come in. You don't have to wait on the porch."

And now she was babbling. She snapped her mouth shut. Turning, she let the door open so he could choose whether he wanted to wait on the porch, or come in. Whatever.

She turned the slow cooker down and headed out.

He leaned against the door jam, straightening as she approached.

"You sure it's not a problem to wait?"

"I'd like to get the fence done."

He didn't move from the doorway. "How are your hands?"

"Fine," she said.

His lips pursed. He remained in her way.

Fine. She held her hands out, palms up.

He hissed through his teeth. "You still have the gloves I gave you?"

"Yes."

He expelled a thoughtful breath. "I'm gonna need someone to hold the rails. Do you think you can?"

"Yes."

His lips flattened, but he didn't say more, moving so she could go through the door and close it. They stepped off the small porch.

Snickers hopped out along with them.

"You can ride with me; I'll drive us down."

"I'm afraid Snickers might get hit."

"He can get in, too."

She hadn't been sure he'd let the dog in his truck. "Okay. Thanks."

Oddly, he came over to the passenger side along with her, and she wondered what in the world he was going to do. Surely he hadn't meant for her to drive?

But he opened the passenger door and looked at her.

She assumed it meant she was supposed to get in. Her mouth dropped. Had anyone ever opened her door for her?

"Is it dirty?" He looked around the door, like his pickup would somehow look different than it had three minutes ago when he'd parked it.

"You're opening the door for me."

Wariness settled over his features. "You're one of those women who yell at men who open doors for them?"

"I'm one of those women who's never met a man who wanted to open a door for me."

He stared at her. His brows went up and he grunted. Then one side of his mouth turned up in the lopsided grin she had started to love when they put the posts in.

"Guess you just did," he murmured, still smiling.

Why did she have such a hard time pulling her eyes away from his? Her breaths came in shaky bursts and her heart seemed to beat extra loud in her chest.

Snickers whined at her feet, and she broke away from his gaze.

"Come on, girl." She climbed up on her seat and Snickers jumped up on her lap.

McKoy's eyes still sparkled as he closed her door.

What was she thinking? He was the dog catcher. A government employee. Totally off limits to her. And yet her eyes tracked his progress as he walked around the front of his truck. She had to force herself to look away as he opened the door and got in.

He drove slowly to the barn. "How's the elephant doing?"

Oh, yeah. He was supposed to be keeping track of that, too. He wasn't here for a social visit.

"I think she's a little depressed."

He quirked a brow in her direction. "Depressed?" His tone said he didn't believe it.

"Yeah. She was always with her sister. They were never apart. Not for anything. And now she's alone."

"Hmm."

"Elephants are actually very intelligent. They do have feelings, as hard as it might be to believe."

"Gotta say, it sounds a little far-fetched to me, but I've never been around an elephant before and you apparently spent your life with them, so I guess that makes you the expert." He turned the truck toward the barn.

"Really?"

Lines appeared between his brows as he looked over at her. "Yeah. Of course. What do I know about elephants?"

She stared at the dash, shaking her head. One would never hear a Mexican official admitting they were not the expert in anything. At least in her experience. And McKoy's job was as an animal control officer. She couldn't believe he was admitting that she, a Mexican with no education, who didn't even belong here, was the expert. Of course, he didn't know she didn't belong in the country.

"You probably won't ever run into this situation again, but I can teach you a little." She gripped her fingers in Snicker's fur. "If you want, of course."

"I'd love to learn."

He sounded sincere.

"Then I'll do it. You already aren't afraid of her. That's important, because they can sense that."

"Apparently you can too."

"Sense that you're not afraid?"

He nodded.

"Of course. You were leery, especially before you knew I knew her, but you were never afraid."

He stopped at the gate and she opened her door. "I didn't realize you were watching me."

"I had to."

Her eyes widened, shocked that she had allowed that to come out, and she almost popped a hand over her mouth. Instead, she jumped out. Snickers landed beside her and she closed the door before he could ask about her odd statement.

Chapter 8

McKoy hadn't forgotten what Jillian had said by the time the last rail was fitted and attached.

Why had she felt she "had" to watch him? To protect her elephant? Surely she knew he wouldn't hurt it. But nothing else made sense. Unless she thought he was going to hogtie the beast and throw it in the back of his pickup, hauling it down to the shelter.

Maybe.

In his experience, women weren't always logical. His mother certainly hadn't been, choosing to leave his hard-working, steady father to chase after some hard-drinking, big partying man. She wasn't with that guy anymore, but she never had come home. Eventually his dad had found another woman and moved to Florida to marry her. She'd left him as well. His dad had said he wasn't moving again.

Still, for Jillian, it seemed like an odd thing to say, and the expression on her face meant she hadn't meant to say it.

She had been wary of him at first, but he assumed it was because of his job. He thought she'd been getting more comfortable and realizing that he was a human, just like her. Nothing to be afraid of.

But maybe that wasn't it. Could she be being nice to him to try to get special favors because of her elephant?

Not the fence. He'd volunteered to do that himself. But maybe that gave her the idea?

If not, why did she feel she "had" to watch him? And why didn't she want him to know? He didn't know the answers, and he wasn't sure he wanted to. He preferred thinking that she kind of liked him. Nothing beyond friendship, of course, but he could handle being friends with someone like Jillian.

She'd pulled her weight this afternoon, despite her sore hands. He'd tried to make sure she didn't do anything to hurt them more, but she had resisted his efforts to give her easy jobs. He admired that.

"McKoy. Come here."

He put the last of his tools in his toolbox, and slammed the lid shut. The sun had settled below the mountain, but it was still light enough to see.

He stepped under the barn roof.

"Walk slow." Jillian's voice, with its lilting accent, came from back in the corner.

He followed her command, arriving at her side as she stroked the elephant's trunk.

"Her head is hanging down some, and her ears aren't up. They're kind of droopy. That's what makes me think she's depressed. That and—see her eyes? It looks like there are tears in them."

He couldn't really tell about the head, but he could see that the ears weren't flapping back and forth, but kind of hung down. He also could see that her eyes, did indeed, seem to have tears.

"Interesting. And you think she's missing her sister?"

"I'm almost sure of it."

"What are you going to do about it?"

"I want to find her."

"You're going to have two elephants?" He could hardly believe it.

"No. I can't afford to feed one. Maybe the person who has her sister wants another. Or maybe whoever sold her sister to him knows someone else who would like an elephant."

"Hmm. Well, the second idea seems like a possibility, but if whoever bought her sister wanted a second elephant, he probably would have gotten them both together."

"Unless they weren't together when he bought them. I'd want to see where he's keeping her and how he's treating her anyway. But you're probably right." She stroked the trunk again. "Would you like to touch her?"

"I know you said I wasn't afraid, but I do remember hearing horror stories about elephants who attacked their handler or went berserk in a crowd."

"She's not really acting like herself, and any wild animal is unpredictable, but I wouldn't suggest it if I thought there was going to be a problem. She normally loves attention."

"Okay." He wasn't sure about this, but he trusted her.

"Give me your hand." She held her own hand out, palm up.

He placed his hand in hers. It was warm and rough. She used both of her hands to hold it. Moving Heidi's trunk gently, she helped Heidi sniff McKoy's hand. Her trunk patted up his arm, and over his face and hair.

He held himself frozen in place. She hadn't even had to tell him to be still. But she could see his teeth gleam in the dim light.

Softly, she said, "It feels weird, doesn't it?"

"I'm just hoping it doesn't feel like lunch to her."

Jillian chuckled low. "I think she likes you. You can pet her now."

He ran his hand over her front shoulder, as high as he could reach. "I expected her to feel rougher."

"Like sandpaper?"

"Yeah. Exactly. It's rough, but not grainy."

"Like nothing we've ever felt before." She'd missed working with the elephants. Hadn't really thought she'd ever touch one again. There was something special about sharing her love with McKoy.

"Doesn't it hurt your hands to touch her?" he asked.

"A little."

Just then his stomach growled.

"Oh, I'm sorry. Sometime you're here in the daylight, and we're not building fence, I'll show you some of the things Heidi and I can do together."

"I'd love to see it. You guys had your own act?"

"Yes. With Hazel, her sister." She stepped away, and McKoy followed.

"You trained them?"

"Not completely. I worked under the trainer, but Heidi and her sister were my special project. I worked out a reward system that seemed to work with them."

"Interesting. I've never met an elephant trainer before." His words seemed to echo hers where she said she'd never had anyone open her car door before.

"Elephant trainer might be a little much. Heidi and her sister are the only two I've worked with."

They'd reached the truck, and she walked ahead to open the gate while he jumped in. After he drove through and she closed it, she looked around for Snickers. He'd just been there, following at their heels as they walked to the truck, but she didn't see him.

Opening the door to tell McKoy she'd walk and keep an eye out for her dog, she saw Snickers sitting on the seat, right beside McKoy, looking out the windshield like he was helping to drive.

"Oh. I was looking for him." She nodded at her dog, interested in the way Snickers had taken to McKoy. Snickers was a stray she'd picked up around Christmastime, and she didn't do well with strangers and men in particular. But McKoy wasn't exactly a stranger after spending two afternoons and evenings with them.

"I think he wants to drive," McKoy said, giving Snickers a pat on the head. Snickers leaned into him, and Jillian could hardly believe that her dog that hated men was cuddled up to McKoy.

She climbed in and Snickers barely noticed. She certainly didn't seem to care if Jillian was with her or not.

Back when she was young, different people at the circus had said dogs and kids could always tell if a person was good. If that was true, Snickers had chosen McKoy as a "good" person.

It seemed like something inside of Jillian had chosen the same thing.

They stopped at her little house, and she suddenly felt shy. It would be McKoy and her, alone, in her home together. Her life hadn't exactly been full of private, intimate moments with large, strapping men.

"Come on in," she said as she opened the door, which wasn't locked. "It should be just a few minutes until I put it on the table." A smell, food, but not necessarily a good food smell, filled her house. She hardly ever used her slow cooker, and it smelled like maybe she hadn't turned it down enough.

"What can I do to help?" McKoy asked as he stood behind her, too close, while she washed her hands, which only stung a little, or else she'd gotten used to the pain. Her heart had started to trip along, and suddenly her house felt really small. His presence hadn't bothered her as much when they were outside working. Open spaces, probably.

"There's tea in the fridge. You can carry it to the table."

"Okay." He moved in behind her to wash his hands while she dried hers, carefully.

The smell was worse now, and her stomach cramped. Was she really going to mess this up? The slow cooker was supposed to be easy to use. True, she didn't use it much, but it wasn't that hard to cook some meat, throw some taco seasonings in and put it in the slow cooker.

But as she lifted the lid, the black stuff that had been blurry as she looked through the glass became clear. Her taco meat was charred.

If it were her, she'd have just thrown a sandwich together. But she'd used the last of her cold cuts the day before. She didn't even have any greens for a salad.

She turned, the slow cooker lid still in her hand, wanting to dig her toe into the floor.

Yeah, he was really going to be impressed with her. And after he'd done such a great job of helping her with her fence, she'd wanted him to...like her? To impress him? She wasn't sure, but she did know that at some point, his opinion of her had started to matter.

"Um…"

He looked up from where he'd been setting the tea on the table. "Yeah?" His head tilted.

"I don't think we're going to be able to eat this."

His brows lifted.

She thought he might be trying to hold back a smile.

He walked over and peered in the pot, then nodded. "I thought it might be salvageable, but even the middle is black."

She pulled her lips in, biting them, and nodded.

He straightened. "Can I say this is kind of a relief to me, because my stomach stopped growling as soon as I smelled it?"

Normally she was pretty unflappable, the result of a childhood spent not allowing the previous bad performance to impact the next performance. But although she'd made some pretty embarrassing blunders in front of large crowds, this was the first time in her life she wanted to burrow under the covers and cry.

Everything she did in front of this man made her look incompetent and stupid.

"I'll still feed you, but give me a minute to figure something out." She would have to dip into her business account in order to buy groceries, and she hated to do that until she'd bought all the dog food she needed to feed the kenneled dogs for the week. There was also the possibility that one of her obedience clients would cancel and she'd owe a refund. She needed to keep enough back to cover that. Then, of course, there was Heidi. She'd ordered a load of hay to be delivered tomorrow. She'd have to pay for that too.

There was also rent, which Fink and Ellie didn't require, but she needed to pay for her own peace of mind—she couldn't come to America and be a leech off people who accepted her at her word that they were her relatives and had given her a job and a place to stay and had helped her start a business.

"Hey." McKoy's hand lifted like he was going to touch her, but it dropped. "It's okay. Sometimes things don't work out. Plus, it wasn't really fair that you worked on the fence *and* had to cook supper."

She shook her head, unable to tell him she hated looking incompetent.

"The all-night diner on the other side of Love's isn't bad. Come on." He touched her arm.

It felt like a shock went through her skin and up to her collar bone and she jerked.

"Sorry," he said, like he thought she didn't want to be touched.

"No, it was me." She hated that cliché. She also hated what she had to tell him. "I can't afford to buy supper there."

"Jillian, look at me."

She lifted her eyes for the first time since she'd picked up the lid. His dark blue gaze was kind and she could hardly face the compassion in his eyes.

"It's been fun working with you. I've enjoyed it. I hated that your hands hurt, but I admired that you kept working anyway." He blew out a breath before looking at her again. "If you don't want to go eat with me, that's fine. I don't want you to feel like you have to. But I'm starving and you have to be, too. Let me buy your supper."

She lowered her eyes, shaking her head.

His finger reached out and touched her chin, tilting it up. "Please?"

"I just hate that everything I've done is such a failure."

"I've heard nothing but good things about your dog kenneling business. It's been clean and the dogs well cared for every time I've seen it. Uncle Roy can't say enough good things about you. And I hear about you in town, too." He shrugged. "A few people have said you're odd. I won't name names, but I consider them odd, so it didn't mean much."

She chuckled.

"If you won't go with me, I'll bring you something back. Okay?"

"No, you can't do that."

"I suppose I don't like being told what I can't do anymore than you do." He turned toward the door. "Coming? Or am I bringing something back?"

She hadn't expected him to be so nice. Telling herself that she would pay him back as soon as she had the money, she nodded.

"I'm driving."

"Or else we're walking because I don't have a license or a car, remember?"

He stopped with his hand on her door knob. "I'd forgotten. You'll have to tell me about that. I don't think I know anyone else who doesn't have their driver's license and a car. Not around here."

He held the door and she walked through.

"I'm not originally from here." Oh, there she went again. The truth was always on the tip of her tongue, waiting to hop off.

"I figured with that accent, you came from somewhere exotic."

Her chest tightened. Spending time with this man was dangerous. Time to shift the focus. "Did you grow up here?"

"Yep. Lived in the same house all...my life." His last two words were soft, like he was remembering something and hadn't wanted to admit to living in the same place.

"That sounds wonderful to me. In the circus we moved around so much. I never really had a home. I lived in a tent most of my life. Train cars, some."

"Train cars? That seems old-fashioned. I never saw a travelling circus on a train as I was growing up."

He was just making conversation, but he was coming too close to the secrets that she was trying to keep hidden.

She stopped at the hood of his truck. He'd not gone to his own side, and she figured he was going to open her door again. Her heart sighed at the chivalry, but her brain scolded her to get some barriers between them before she ended up spilling her guts and getting deported back to Mexico. And what would happen to Heidi if that happened?

She stopped short. "Oh, I forgot. I actually have some work I never finished at the kennel. Thanks so much for the offer, but some other time."

"Jillian—"

She hurried off before he could stop her.

She hadn't exactly lied. The pens could always be cleaned. He didn't call her name again, and he didn't follow her. It should have made her happy, but her chest felt empty and cold.

Chapter 9

Monday morning, McKoy sat at his desk, trying to catch up on some paperwork. He avoided his office and desk as much as he could. He'd become an animal control officer because he loved animals and hated sitting inside. This part of the job was his least favorite.

He'd left his door cracked and a tap on it pushed it open farther. Louie walked in with a piece of paper in his hand. Never a good sign. It would be a complaint of some kind.

McKoy waited.

Louie looked over the paper. "I think this is the same address as the elephant."

McKoy's heart skidded to a stop. What had happened?

He'd felt awful that Jillian had admitted to not being able to afford a meal. But it actually made him admire her more. She was obviously feeding her animals quite well. And she was willing to go without in order to keep doing it.

He'd gone to the diner and ordered two meals for takeout. The lights were off in Jillian's house, but he left her container on the banister. It was cool enough it wouldn't spoil. Hopefully she saw it.

Louie browsed the paper some more. "Apparently there was a wedding at the property?"

He nodded. He'd not gone out to inspect Heidi's pen, not only because he'd just been there Friday, but also because of the wedding.

"A little girl got bitten by one of the dogs that were being kenneled. I don't have any more info. You have time today to check this out?"

"Yeah." He pushed back on his chair. He hadn't wanted to do the paperwork anyway. "I'll head out there right now. I have a few more things I need to do anyway."

"Okay. Figured I'd give this one to you because you've been working with the woman." He stopped talking and looked McKoy full in the face. "I know Todd was messing with you some the other day in my office, but you really don't have a thing for her, do you? Because you know I'd need to take you off her case if you do. A man gets tangled up in a relationship and his rational thought suffers."

"No. I'm not having any trouble thinking rationally."

She hadn't wanted to eat with him. That was a pretty big clue that there wasn't any attraction or interest on her end. He'd spent the weekend convincing himself that there was no interest on his end either. It wasn't true, but it was just as well. A woman who'd travelled as Jillian had wouldn't be interested in a homebody like him. He couldn't believe that he'd actually blurted out that he'd lived in the same house all his life. His fiancée hadn't been impressed with that little detail of his life.

"Good." Louie handed McKoy the slip of paper and walked out.

It was a little over a half an hour from the office to Sweet Haven Farm where Jillian's kennel was.

He pulled slowly into the drive, waving at Avery as she walked up the steps to the big farmhouse. She'd be living with Gator, of course, but he thought she was still in charge of the receptions at the barn. She'd have been the one setting things up and supervising on Saturday.

He wanted to talk to Jillian first. The dog was under her care.

He slowed when he went by her small house, but the place looked unoccupied, so he continued on to the kennels.

She was out cleaning them.

Part of his body dreaded having to confront her about the girl's bite, the other part of him jumped up and down in excitement to have an excuse to be near her again.

He stopped and got out. She glanced up, her eyes widening in surprise. She probably hadn't heard him approach over the barking of the dogs.

Her eyes swept down his body and back up, noting the uniform. Wariness leapt into her expression and her chest expanded like she was taking a big breath.

She set the shovel aside and let herself out of the kennel, striding over to him.

He liked that. She wasn't trying to hide, and she didn't make him chase her down, but confronted her problem head-on.

"Hello, Mr. Rodning."

Her soft, musical tone sounded perfect to his ears, but he hated that she put that distance between them with the "mister."

"How's Heidi?"

"She's doing great. I got a load of hay delivered here early Saturday morning, and I'm checking with a couple of tree trimming companies to see if I can get some branches to supplement her diet."

He nodded. That was a great idea. It would probably be free, too. Unlike hay, which was expensive, especially this time of year.

"Glad to hear that. Maybe, since I'm here, I can do the unscheduled visit if it suits you."

She pushed the hair that had escaped from her ponytail back off her face. Her face was flushed from the work she'd been doing and she looked slim in her T-shirt and soft-looking blue jeans. He noted she wore the work gloves he'd bought her. Her hands were probably still tender.

"I don't think it will work today. I have a class starting in about thirty minutes."

He tried for his best professional look. "Okay. I don't want to make you late, but we have a report of a little girl getting bitten by one of your dogs. Can you tell me what happened?"

The wary look on her face intensified, but her voice stayed level and she looked him in the eye. "Sure. She was attending the wedding at the barn with her parents, and she slipped away. Apparently they didn't notice. She came down here and stuck her hand in between the chain link fence." She pointed to what looked like a husky mix. "I don't think the dog meant to hurt her, but he was probably excited."

"Was she bleeding?"

"No. Nothing punctured the skin. There was one small indentation in her finger that could have been made by a tooth, but nothing else." She lifted a shoulder. "I have the parents' number."

"Do you mind giving it to me?"

"Not at all. I told them that they'd probably be getting a call. From my insurance agent, if no one else, because they decided to take her to the ER."

"Okay. Great." So they'd be expecting a call. Hopefully they told the same story Jillian just did. "Thanks." He stood, thinking about whether there was anything else he needed to ask, before he turned to go.

"McKoy?"

His heart flipped at her use of his name. "Yeah?"

"I'm sorry about Friday night."

He didn't say anything. Didn't allow the excited beating of his heart to change the expression on his face. She twisted her hands together before taking her gloves off and slapping them on her leg.

"I ran away and it wasn't nice of me." She bit her lip. "Thanks for the meal. It was my breakfast the next morning."

"You're welcome." He looked over her head, needing to address her apology. "It's probably better that way."

"Yeah."

His phone buzzed and he was tempted not to look at it, but he didn't have anything else to add, so he pulled it out of his pocket.

You might as well let her know that I've gotten two complaints about the elephant. Wedding guests.

McKoy closed his eyes. It seemed like everything was against Jillian. He hated to add to it, but she needed to know.

"This is my boss." He held up his phone, keeping the screen pointed toward him. "People from the wedding must have seen Heidi. They're complaining, apparently. I'm not sure about what, but it doesn't matter. We have to investigate all complaints."

"I see."

"I know you have a class. I can walk down to the barn, make sure she has food and water and that our fence is holding." He got a little thrill out of saying "our" fence, but the dejected set of her shoulders hurt his heart.

She swallowed and nodded. "That's fine."

"You know, Jillian. Not to make your life harder, but it might not be the best idea to have an elephant near where there are going to be wedding guests possibly wandering around. I know she's a very calm animal, but she's big enough that things could get ugly fast."

"I understand." She wouldn't meet his eyes, instead focusing on the gravel under their feet. Her shoulders were turned away, like she wanted to leave but was staying for politeness.

"I'm sorry."

She nodded. "Is that it?"

"Yes." For now.

"Do I need to go to the barn with you?"

He hated to leave her, didn't want to be the person who made her feel bad, but he'd already done more for her than he should. More than Louie would think was acceptable.

"No." He gritted his jaw. "Is there a wedding this Saturday? We can schedule my next visit, since I can count this one as the un-scheduled."

"No. But Wildlife Days are Saturday and Sunday afternoon. I'm doing some presentations. With your uncle's dogs." She looked up, giving him a ghost of a smile.

"That's right." He was giving his own presentation on snakes. "How's Friday?"

"That's fine."

"I'll see you then." He left. Because he had to.

Chapter 10

Tuesday morning, Jillian stopped at Uncle Roy's house to work with his dogs and to check on him. She wasn't sure exactly what McKoy did during the week when he didn't come home, but supposedly it related to his job somehow. Regardless, she enjoyed visiting with Uncle Roy, and she enjoyed working with his dogs as well. They had a nice visit before she jogged to the post office and then back home where her day didn't exactly go as planned.

It didn't surprise Jillian when McKoy's truck came slowly down the drive on Wednesday morning. She'd been expecting it since her confrontation with a student and his handler at her Tuesday night obedience class.

She quit cleaning the pens and waited for him to stop and get out.

"This is getting to be a habit," he said by way of greeting.

If only he weren't here because of more complaints. He looked fabulous in his uniform. Strong and confident. But she knew there was kindness and consideration there as well. The combination was addictive and attractive. She had to remind herself he was off-limits.

"I should get you your own parking space. Put up a sign that says 'This space reserved for animal control officer.'"

He smiled, but it didn't stretch to his eyes.

"I guess you know why I'm here."

She nodded.

"Can you tell me what happened?"

She shoved a hand in her pocket and leaned a shoulder against the metal building. The dogs' barking frenzy had died down enough for him to be able to hear her. "I have a pit bull in my Tuesday night class. I know they have a reputation, but they're actually great with people and really sweet." Dumb, too. But it wasn't really their fault. They'd been bred to fight, not to use their brains. "But he's not so keen on his fellow students. I had to ask his handler to leave, after he started showing aggression toward the Irish wolfhound in the class. I didn't want a dog fight on my hands."

"Of course." McKoy nodded.

"They left, but the handler shouted a few insults on the way out, complaining that the place smells and is dirty. That I'm a fake and fraud." That insult had smarted, because it was so close to the truth. "He said he was going to report me. I have the names and numbers of the other students in the class if you'd like to confirm my story."

"Yeah, I'll take them." His lips pressed together. "We've been getting so many complaints about you that my supervisor is thinking about making a trip out here."

She bit her cheeks. He pulled the ever-present gum out of his pocket.

She gave a shaky laugh before taking a piece.

"Is that something I should worry about? Your supervisor coming out?"

One side of his mouth pulled back and he crossed his arms over his chest. "He's not happy about the elephant not having a permit. He's on me to push you about it. Legally you have thirty days. But..." He shrugged. "I want to say that my supervisor would do the exact same things I'm doing, but I'm not sure that's true." He lifted a shoulder.

Jillian didn't need him to tell her Louie wouldn't come and help her make her fence. He wouldn't have offered to buy her supper. Maybe McKoy *was* playing favorites.

Jillian bit her cheeks despite the gum he'd given her. His chest tightened. She pulled something deep inside of him. Whatever it was, it made him feel protective of her. It also drove him to seek her out, to run his eyes over her face, to want to touch her and make her life easier.

He didn't want to give up his authority to Louie, and especially not to Todd. McKoy wanted to be the one to be here for Jillian.

Maybe that was a good reason for him to walk away.

"But should I worry about him coming out?" Jillian asked again.

"I'm going to do what I can, and no, you don't need to worry."

Something like relief eased the lines in her face. He only hoped he could live up to that promise.

Saturday was a beautiful, warm day. The forsythia bushes were in full bloom, early tulips and late daffodils colored lawns while the grass was an almost electric shade of green.

Fresh, new earth scented the air, even over the roasting hot dogs and fried food smells that soaked through the town of Love.

It was Wildlife Days, and Love didn't do small celebrations.

Enough people milled around that Love could almost be mistaken for Pittsburgh, minus the hills and rivers and skyscrapers.

Jillian would never confuse the small town she'd fallen in love with, with a big city, though. Everyone knew almost everyone else, and if they didn't, they smiled and greeted each other anyway.

Sure, she was looked on with a bit of suspicion, since she wasn't born and raised in the area, or maybe she would be looked at like that no matter where she went.

At any rate there were a ton of people gathered around as she held onto Chatty and Bubbles. Snickers was off-leash, sitting under a "stay" command. One could never be a hundred percent sure about how an animal was going to behave, but Jillian had as much confidence as a person could have in Snickers.

Uncle Roy sat in a lawn chair in the front row. Jillian had offered to see if Avery or Ellie would pick him up, but he'd said McKoy was coming and would bring him.

Sure enough, thirty minutes before she was scheduled to begin, Uncle Roy had hobbled over, his dogs on leash. McKoy walked beside him carrying the lawn chair.

Their eyes met, his dark and brooding, but a small smile had tilted his lips up. She had to return it. The air had seemed to sizzle around them, and the noise of the townspeople faded as they became the only two people in the world for several long seconds.

Uncle Roy had said something and broken the spell, but Jillian was having a harder and harder time convincing herself that there was nothing between herself and McKoy. What wasn't hard was convincing herself it wouldn't last. She knew nothing could ever come of it.

Jillian tried to get her mind off McKoy, who was somewhere nearby doing something with his job. Maybe Uncle Roy had mentioned snakes.

Several small children gathered around Bubbles and Chatty, petting them while the dogs tried to lick their faces and snuggle up. They loved the attention and were great with the kids. Jillian bent down, answering questions and making sure the smallest children weren't pushed over.

She took a second to check her watch. The parade was over, more people were gathering and it was time to start her demonstration.

"Okay, we're going to get started." This was much better than the circus, where she had to wear a frilly costume and everything was done to the beat of fast-paced music.

People settled back and Uncle Roy smiled from the front.

As she put the dogs through the tricks she'd taught them, she explained several main principles of training. People seemed interested, and she hoped it helped them as they worked on training their own dogs.

The most popular part of her demonstration seemed to be when she combined her contortionist routine with the dogs' obedience. Maybe because people didn't typically see that. Whatever the reason, when she was finished, people begged to see them again. The dogs were game, so she obliged the crowd.

Instead of working an hour, she ended up doing two hours of demonstrations, another hour of questions and more tricks. She had a feeling the audience at the end was an entirely different audience than at the beginning, because who could watch that long? But they were just as engaged, which warmed her chest and made her feel light and bubbly inside.

Uncle Roy watched the whole time. After telling the audience she was really done this time, she walked over to him.

"What'd you think?"

"I think you're the best thing that's ever happened at Wildlife Days." His whiskered face split into a grin. "I think I even learned some things, and they were my dogs." He shook his head. "I can't believe they were my dogs. Why can't I get them to do that stuff at home?"

She smiled. "I know you can. It just takes practice. The more you work with them, the better you understand them, and they understand you."

"Sounds like a marriage to me," the old man said with a twinkle in his eye.

Jillian kept her smile, although part of her had despaired of ever getting married. "I don't have any experience in that area."

"I can tell you it ain't easy." He rubbed his hand over his face. "Mabel and I couldn't have kids, then God took her early. Guess I'm kind of glad McKoy's parents had such a hard time, and he ended up with me."

Jillian couldn't deny she was curious. "Someone said he'd lived in your house all his life?"

"Yeah, I bought the house from his parents about twenty years ago. About when Mabel died. His mom ran off, and his dad was struggling. He has sisters, you know."

No, Jillian hadn't known.

"They didn't stick around, either. Looking for something more exciting than this one-horse town."

"So he's the only steady one in his family?"

"My little brother, his dad, isn't bad. But he moved to Florida to be with his new wife and family. She left him, but he doesn't want to come back." He patted Chatty, who had made herself at home in his lap.

She really wanted to hear more about McKoy's family, but he probably wouldn't appreciate her digging.

"Do you want to walk around a little?" she offered.

"Nah." He kept his hand moving on his dog's head. "I've seen all this a hundred times. McKoy's coworker is relieving him in a few minutes. I'll go home with him."

Someone tapped her on the shoulder. "Do you think you could teach my dog to do all that stuff?"

She turned, her response natural on her lips. "Sure. Pretty much any dog can learn the basics."

The girl, maybe in her late teens, nodded.

Jillian realized there was a line of people waiting to ask her questions. She hadn't expected this. "Let me pour some water for Snickers, and come over here so I can sit down."

With a last look at Uncle Roy, who appeared to be in good shape, Jillian led the line over to the small, make-shift platform she'd used for her demonstration. She poured some of the water she'd brought into Snicker's bowl, and the dog lapped at it.

People gathered around her when she sat down, and peppered her with questions. She was in the middle of an explanation of the best house-training practices when she noticed McKoy come for Uncle Roy. He glanced over at her and their eyes met, but she looked away immediately. She would never be able to answer questions if she spent all her time staring at his rugged jaw and wide shoulders.

The crowd had thinned, her stomach was crying in hunger, and she'd answered more questions than she'd ever thought she could when the hair on the back of her neck pricked up and she noticed McKoy standing off to her right with his arms crossed over his chest, his legs braced. Her heart stuttered at the handsome picture, but her brain warned her that if he wanted to talk to her, it probably wasn't good.

Her stomach forgot about being hungry and commenced nervous cramping. Now what? More complaints?

She finished speaking to the lady in front of her. Before anyone else could ask her anything, McKoy materialized by her right elbow.

"She's done for now, folks. The lady hasn't eaten anything today and she looks like she's ready to fall over. You can find her at Fink and Ellie's if you want to talk to her." McKoy's voice was kind, yet firm, and folks good-naturedly moved away.

She crossed her arms and tapped her foot. "That was presumptuous of you."

"Yeah." He looked at her with the look that could melt stone.

Her body was not immune, but she tried to resist. "You're not going to apologize?"

"No." His breathing was steady, and his eyes didn't flinch.

"I think you should." Her voice didn't come out like she wanted it to. Rather, it was more of a whisper.

"You are hungry. You are tired. And you need a break." His lips flattened. "There's nothing to apologize for."

"I can make these decisions on my own." She was arguing for no good reason. It was actually nice to have someone take care of her. The circus had been like one big family, and she missed that aspect. But she had always been on her own with taking care of herself.

McKoy swallowed and his eyes moved to a point over her shoulder. "I'm sorry. You look exhausted." His eyes met hers again. "Walk with me for a bit and let me get you something to eat."

Her stomach spun like a cotton candy machine. She should tell him no. She should leave. There was plenty of work to do at home, even though she'd cancelled her Saturday classes because of the festival.

"Okay."

His lip curved up. "Really? No argument? You must be pretty hungry."

"I am. How did you know I hadn't eaten all day?"

"Just figured."

He knew the state of her bank account, although she'd bought the hay and dog food and cut a rent check. She had a little bit left. She could buy groceries. Rice and beans. She'd grown up on them. With the right spices, they were delicious. And cheap.

"We taking Snickers with us?" he asked.

She eyed the dog, sleeping beside the platform, sprawled out in the sun. "I'd better bring her with me."

"Leash?"

"She'll be fine. Snickers, heel."

Snickers jumped up, did a quick stretch, and came to Jillian's side. Jillian dug in her pocket for her last treat.

"We're ready," she said.

"What do you feel like?" McKoy asked, waiting for her to come to his side before starting to stroll to where all the food vendors were set up.

"Anything I don't have to kill first."

He looked at her oddly. She wanted to slap her hand over her mouth and take it back. Even when she lived in Mexico, they didn't usually have to kill their food and dress it before they cooked it, but it wasn't such a foreign idea that it would garner a look like McKoy had just given her. She'd meant it as a joke.

His lips curved up. "I was over with the rattlesnakes. I've heard they're good, but they're out of season. Don't think it would do for me to be making them lunch."

"I'm not hungry for snake anyway."

"That's nice. I wouldn't know how to cook it. And," he eyed her with a raised brow, "I'm not sure I want you to."

"Wow. Really? I burn one meal, one time, and he's going to rub it in forever."

"It was well beyond the burnt stage. Charred. Mummified. So burnt the dogs wouldn't even eat it."

She put a hand up. "Okay. I get the picture. I always figure there's no point in doing something halfway."

"Yep. There was no halfway about it. It was burnt the whole way through."

"So you're a great cook?" she asked. There was no way she was winning that argument. He wasn't wrong about how badly she'd burnt it.

"Passable, I'd say. I can make coffee. Boil pasta. Grill hamburgers." He tilted his head. "Is there anything else?"

"Cemita with milanesa, pozole, Cochinita pibil." And suddenly she realized she was being way too transparent. "French fries."

He snorted.

Gah. She tried to move on, but he remained motionless, his head tilted to the side.

"So, I don't think your accent is purely Spanish, but I'm assuming you speak the language, since you said those things, whatever they are, with what sounded like native authenticity to me."

Yeah. How could he not pick up on that?

"Hey, hot sausage. I could go for a sandwich." She pointed to the nearest booth. Hot sausage wasn't her favorite, but it made McKoy's eyes light up, and he finally started moving again.

They stepped in line, which wasn't overly long, since the lunch rush had ended hours ago.

"Should we get something for Snickers?" McKoy asked.

"I think she's fine. She ate this morning before we came and I just gave her a drink of water."

After checking to see if she wanted a drink, he stepped up and ordered them both a sandwich and a water along with a large order of cheese fries.

After the vendor handed them their food, McKoy said, "If you don't mind walking a bit, there's a pretty spot by the river that won't be crowded. After your busy morning, I'd assume you could use a quiet break."

Could she ever. She'd never thought she would be busy performing and answering questions all that time. "Thank you. I don't mind at all."

She followed him past the booths and tables, Snickers at her heel. It was only five minutes or so when they'd rounded a small hill and reached the rocky edge of the river. Several rocks made a perfect natural seat, and the green grass and budding trees contrasted with the bright blue sky to make the spot idyllic.

"I didn't even realize this was here," she said as they situated themselves on the rocks facing each other, the river beside them.

"Yeah, it's pretty."

It felt odd to her that McKoy would bring her to such a pretty spot. Their relationship had been contentious for the most part. But he kept surprising her with his kindness and consideration. Maybe the contention was mostly on her part. Contention and attraction. She couldn't seem to find the happy middle ground that McKoy walked so easily. She vowed to do better.

She had eaten two bites of her sandwich before she blurted out, "Do you bring a lot of girls here?"

His eyes snapped to hers. They widened before his lip pulled back, like he was resigned to divulge information he didn't necessarily want to talk about. "I was engaged in college. It ended badly, kind of like my parents, only we weren't married. I've been focused on my job since."

She nodded. She hadn't really meant anything about her and him, necessarily. Just if this was something he did regularly. She didn't want to be one of many. Not with McKoy. But she didn't really understand what made her feel that way, so she let the subject drop.

"How's the permit process going?" he asked.

She stared at her sandwich, her insides rioting. "Fine," she said. She took a fry and popped it into her mouth.

The permit process wasn't happening at all, because it said right on the website that one had to be a citizen to even apply. She hadn't gotten any phone numbers from her contacts in Mexico, but she wouldn't stop working on it. In fact, as soon as she got home, she would call again. She didn't want McKoy to get in trouble when the thirty days were up and she hadn't even applied. Heidi needed to have a home before then.

"It's a beautiful day. Let's forget about elephant problems for a while. Sound good?" McKoy asked.

There was something in his eyes that made her want to forget about all her problems and just enjoy a pretty day with a handsome man. She was tempted to forget who he was and what she wasn't.

"I figured you brought me back here so you could grill me in private." She eased the words with a smile, but they still were designed to put a wall between them.

"I brought you here because you're working hard and you need a break." McKoy looked out over the water. "And because it's pretty and so are you."

Her eyes widened. He'd complimented her. McKoy wasn't the kind of guy to sweet talk a girl when he didn't mean it. But what did he mean, exactly?

She inclined her head, trying to ignore her speeding heart. "Thanks."

He eased his legs out, angling them away from her, and crossed them. "I did a lot of fishing from these rocks when I was a kid."

"You probably walked here every day." His house wasn't far away.

"Just about." He smiled at her. "Brought my dog with me. Babe. She wasn't half as good-looking as you."

She thought he was flirting with her. "I'm better looking than your dog? I'll take it, I guess." She tossed her pony tail over her shoulder and decided to throw her naturally cautious nature over her shoulder with it. "You definitely have nicer shoulders than Snickers."

"Shoulders?" He laughed out loud. "I'm not even sure Snickers has shoulders, so I don't know what that means."

"That means I can't look at your shoulders without wanting to touch them."

His laugh stopped abruptly.

She had done it again. Said too much.

Their eyes met and held. His smoldering.

Her heart trembled. She couldn't take the words back, and maybe she didn't want to, anyway. Because she liked the look on his face. The one that said her words had affected him. In a good way.

He leaned toward her, close enough that their breaths mingled. "You know you can touch them anytime you want to."

Why couldn't she breathe? And suddenly her throat was dry, too. "I didn't know."

"I'm telling you."

Her fingers dug into her palm, itching to move toward the wide shoulders that were so close.

"I don't want to get you in trouble," she whispered.

His lips barely moved. His eyes never strayed from hers. "I think it might be worth it."

Her eyes widened.

He moved back just a bit. "But maybe you didn't mean it."

She reached out to stop him. Her hand settled on his bicep.

One side of his mouth kicked up. "You missed."

"Maybe I'm taking the scenic route." Her fingers curled into the hard ridges. "Maybe I'm not allowed to touch this?"

His breath came out shaky. "I think I'd be hard-pressed to tell you no about anything."

"I think that was a yes."

"That was a yes, please."

Her hands slid up his arms and curled around his shoulders. They were as hard as she'd thought they would be. Hot, too.

And suddenly she was drowning in his eyes, moving closer. Instead of touching his shoulders, her hands were moving around them and his lips were close, moving closer.

His eyes were dark and hooded. His muscles rippled under her hand.

Her heart pounded up her throat and she touched her tongue to her dry lip.

A sound like a growl escaped his lips and he moved.

Snickers whined.

Chapter 11

They froze.

"Hey, McKoy. This sure makes it look like you were lying in the office the other day." Todd came strutting around the bend and started down the hill. "You know, that day when you said you didn't have a thing for the elephant lady?"

McKoy searched Jillian's eyes. They were wide, startled, but it didn't look like she regretted what they'd been about to do. He hoped the regret didn't come later.

It wouldn't for him. The only thing he'd regret would be that he didn't actually get to kiss her.

Even now he wanted to pull her to his side and shield her from Todd and whatever venom he was going to spew. But when he'd given her permission to touch him, more like begged her to touch him, she hadn't responded in kind. He didn't know what that meant, other than he wasn't going to put his hands where they weren't wanted.

Her hands slid off his shoulders. His breath hitched. Her eyes widened and darkened as she caught the sound.

The flare of her eyes sent an answering spark through his soul and he was hard pressed to move back.

Then a worry line settled between her brows. He put his thumb up to smooth it out.

"It's okay."

"I don't want you to get in trouble."

"I'm not working. I can be with whomever I want to be with now."

"They might take you off my case."

A real possibility. But he wasn't going to let it happen without a fight. "I don't think so."

He straightened up and turned toward Todd, who was closing the last twenty yards between them. "You lost?"

"It's a public area. Maybe I wanted to come down and see the love birds."

McKoy ground his back teeth together and didn't say anything.

"I think Louie would be interested in hearing about this."

McKoy shrugged.

"If you take yourself out of contention for the supervisor position, I won't tell him." Todd hooked his thumbs in his pockets.

"There's nothing to tell. It's a Saturday afternoon, and I'm spending it with Jillian. There's no law against it, and I'm not breaking any rules."

"Louie will take you off her case."

Jillian moved back. He wanted to reassure her, to put his arm around her and draw him close to his side, but he resisted, giving Todd a casually disinterested glance instead.

"I think not, but I'm not going to argue about it. Tell him what you need to. She's in the process of getting the permit, and that's a black and white deal."

Todd narrowed his eyes. "You have the inspections to do."

"Louie's planning on going out. He'll see what I've been seeing. Everything is neat and well taken care of. One of the best places I've ever seen."

"Or your opinion is biased."

"It's not," McKoy said flatly. "Aren't you supposed to be supervising the snake exhibit?"

"Louie came and said he'd do it for a bit." He turned. "I'd watch my step if I were you."

"I'm not doing anything wrong," McKoy stated again.

"That's a matter of opinion." Todd walked back the way he'd come.

McKoy watched him disappear around the bend, before turning back to Jillian. "Sorry about that."

"It'd be awful to have to work with him every day." She wrinkled her nose.

He hooked a hand around his neck. "It's not been bad. They kind of pitted us against each other with the promotion, and that's sparked a competition. Plus, we don't spend much time together. The department is spread pretty thin and we go out solo most of the time."

"You really want the promotion?"

"It would enable me to be home every night. Uncle Roy is getting to the point where he can't stay by himself. I think he'd go to a retirement community, but he doesn't want to leave Bubbles and Chatty." He supposed they weren't going to talk about their almost-kiss, even though that was the top thing on his mind, far more than dogs or Uncle Roy or even his job. Which probably meant he shouldn't be thinking about it at all.

Because there was no room in his life for a woman.

But why not?

Maybe Jillian was the only woman in the world who didn't think he was too boring to be with. She liked his shoulders, of all things. That was a start.

"He's pretty attached to them."

It took McKoy a minute to remember where they were in their conversation. His uncle's dogs. "They keep him company when I'm gone."

She looked out over the water. A million questions ran through his head. He wanted to find out everything about her. Why she spoke Spanish. Where she grew up. What she did in the circus. He could listen to her talk all day.

But Todd had broken the spell that she'd been under anyway, because she picked up her garbage and said, "I'd better get back up. Thanks so much for the food."

She started to stand.

"Jillian?"

She blinked and her gaze landed somewhere near his collar bone.

"You looking at my shoulders again?" he couldn't help but tease.

A little smile tugged up the corners of her mouth. "Maybe," she said softly.

"Don't leave." Even to him, it sounded like begging.

"It's for the best."

"You can tell me you don't feel anything?" He motioned between them.

"It doesn't matter what I do or don't feel." She lifted a shoulder and shook her head. "It just wouldn't work."

His heart beat like he'd come face to face with a bear. "I think it would."

"There are things that will keep us apart." She clenched her hands in her lap.

"What? Tell me what?"

"I can't."

He put his hand over top of hers. "I can't overcome the problems I don't know exist."

"This isn't anything you can do anything about."

"You can't tell me? Or you won't?" Frustration made his words harsher than he intended. He finally found a woman that seemed perfect. He admired her work ethic, her drive and determination, her compassion for the animals in her care where she'd go hungry to feed them. And she was so beautiful she made his eyes hurt.

She seemed to like him okay earlier.

He bent his head, trying to catch her eye. She finally looked at him. "Tell me you don't feel anything. Tell me you don't want this." He held his hand up, cupping hers. His voice lowered. "Tell me you didn't want me to kiss you earlier."

She swallowed, biting her lip. Her eyes seemed to fill with tears, but they didn't spill out. He felt a pang of guilt for pushing her to that point, but he wouldn't stay where he wasn't welcome. The problem was, he didn't think he wasn't welcome.

"Tell me," he growled.

"I can't," she cried out.

"Why not?" he asked, frustration clear in his voice.

"You're a government employee. I. Can't. Tell. You." She enunciated each word clearly.

Before he could process what that meant, she jumped up, ripping her hands away, and hurried up the hill.

McKoy sat there, stunned. Sometimes women were a mystery to him. But this seemed pretty clear. Jillian was doing something illegal.

Saturday night, after Jillian fed all her dogs and Heidi and cleaned their pens, she spent half an hour on the phone trying to figure something out. She couldn't tell McKoy that she hadn't even started the permit process. He'd been so sure of her. He was risking his position at work by his faith in her. She hated that she wasn't what he thought she was.

Her body still trembled when she thought of how close he'd come to kissing her. Her hands still tingled with the feel of his shoulders and arms. She hated that he'd practically begged her to give them a chance. It had been one of the hardest things she'd ever done to not give in and pretend that she wasn't hiding everything she was from him.

Part of her wanted to go to him and ask for another chance. Surely he wasn't looking at a long-term commitment anyway. The problem was, she couldn't have a fling with McKoy. He was the kind of man a woman wanted to hold on to. Marry. Have a family with.

That was probably not what he was looking for. After he found the truth out about her, it definitely wasn't what he would want with her, anyway.

She sat outside on her porch, listening to the peepers down at the pond and watching the full moon track across the sky. The air was heavy and warm, feeling like thunderstorms might go by in the night. A beautiful night to share with someone.

What was McKoy doing?

She shook her head and tried the number Carlos had given her one last time. Supposedly a millionaire in Brazil had bought Hazel, and this was supposed to be his number. No luck so far.

But it was better for her to keep trying and get sent to a voice mail that hadn't been set up than for her to sit here dreaming about McKoy and what would never happen between them. What she couldn't allow to happen.

"Hello?" The cultured male voice startled her.

"*Bueno*, uh, hello?" she said, startled, because she wasn't expecting anyone to answer. "This is Jillian Powell. I've been told you bought an elephant, a former performer in the Mexican circus. Hazel." She hadn't planned what to say and it was coming out all wrong.

"Who did you say this was?" the voice asked, with more of an English accent than Spanish.

"Jillian Powell. I used to work with the elephants in the circus. Hazel, specifically, and her sister, Heidi."

"Yes. I've seen pictures of you. Very beautiful." Maybe Italian. She couldn't quite place it, but supposed it didn't matter.

"Do you have Hazel?" she asked, unable to wait any longer.

"Yes. I do, actually. And I've been busy, but I wanted to get in touch with you. I was told you handled the elephants."

"Yes." The idea that he had wanted to get in touch with her surprised her into silence.

"I have an elephant, but I do not know how to work with her. She is lazy and just stands around." His voice held frustration.

Jillian's stomach turned over slowly. Hopefully he hadn't taken his frustration out on Hazel. "She might be depressed. She and her sister were inseparable."

"I see." She heard a tapping in the background, like he was drumming his fingers on a desk. "How long will this depression last?"

"I don't know if she'll ever get over it. Elephants have very long memories."

"Hmm. If I could find her sister, would she remember her?"

Excitement flashed through Jillian. She held her voice steady and tried to sound intelligent. "Yes. She would. Elephants are different than a lot of animals that way."

"Interesting."

She gathered up her nerve. "I actually was calling because I have her sister, who is suffering from the same type of depression that you've described for Hazel." Jillian stood up, knowing the next few minutes could mean the difference between having a home for Heidi or not. "I hoped that you might be interested in a second elephant."

There was silence on the other end of the line. "I will have to think about that. While I do, maybe you will think about coming to work for me, taking care of my elephant. Maybe taking care of my two elephants."

She didn't want to turn him down flat, although she had no interest in going to Brazil.

"My name is Mario, by the way. If I were beside you, I would take your hand and kiss it."

Ugh. Thankfully there was a lot of real estate between the two of them. Of course she didn't say that. The only time she really had trouble controlling her mouth was when she looked into McKoy's deep blue eyes. Then her tongue seemed to flap in the breeze while her brain took a vacation.

"How long do you think you'll need to think about whether or not you'll take Heidi?" She wanted this too bad to be coy.

"How long do you think you'll need to think about whether or not you'll come and be my animal trainer?" A few beats of silence ticked by before he added, "I have several different kinds of wild animals on my estate. Do you have experience in anything other than elephants?"

She'd worked with everything from the dogs to the lions to tigers and bears in the circus, but she wasn't comfortable with any of them aside from the dogs and her sister elephants. She didn't want to get into that with Mario.

"No." She left it at that.

"Too bad. Still, my elephant needs a gentle hand. It sounds like you just might be the woman for the job. I could send my private jet up for you."

"I'll need some time to think about it."

"One week?"

He hadn't talked salary or where she would live or anything. But as she thought about it, she figured, why not? Her business here was barely started, so it wasn't like she would be losing much. It might be worth it if she could be with Hazel and Heidi.

She'd have to check Mario out. See if anyone she knew, knew him and could give her the low down.

Even as she thought about it, she could hardly stand the idea of leaving McKoy. She wasn't legal. He would hate her when he found out, but it didn't matter. She couldn't stop herself from not wanting to leave. Because of him.

Chapter 12

T he next Tuesday, McKoy stopped in at Sweet Haven Farm. It was his last stop before being done for the day. He'd planned it that way so he might possibly spend a little time with Jillian.

She was attracted to him. She admitted that much. Maybe she would tell him the "horrible" thing that she was doing that wasn't legal. He could hardly believe it was as bad as she made it out to be. And maybe she had gotten the same idea as his ex-fiancée—that he was boring. Maybe she thought her having the elephant without a permit was enough to put him off.

Not likely.

But that was illegal. He was close to convincing himself that was it.

As he drove down past the house, he could see Heidi was out. Jillian was on her back. A small crowd of people stood back by the gate, watching.

McKoy recognized Gator standing with his arm around Avery. She leaned into him, and they couldn't have looked happier or more in love. Fink held Ellie in much the same way while their three boys stood as still as he'd ever seen them stand, watching Jillian as she rode Heidi around the fenced barnyard. She'd placed haybales in a crude circle, and Heidi followed the outline around.

As they watched, Jillian stood, then slowly bent over backwards. She lifted one foot in the air, then two, doing a split, then latching a foot in the harness and slowly dropping down until she hung completely by her foot along the elephant's front leg.

Heidi kept walking along at a steady pace.

McKoy's heart was in his throat. He wanted to rush down and yank her off. What she was doing was dangerous and foolish.

But she wouldn't appreciate it and he wouldn't do it, even if he could.

So, instead, he parked and walked slowly over to the gate, going to the open spot between Fink and Gator, and propping his foot on the bottom rail.

"Hey, McKoy," Gator greeted him.

He returned Fink's quiet "hello" then leaned toward Gator, keeping his eyes glued on Jillian, who now had Heidi stopped as she stood on her trunk and wrapped her leg around it. Heidi lifted her up, and Jillian let go, bending backwards, holding on with only her toes.

McKoy could hardly stand to watch. Without looking away, he asked, "How are the love birds?"

"Doing good." Gator gave a genuine grin.

McKoy slapped him on the back. "Glad to hear it."

They watched in silence a few more minute until Jillian finally climbed down and led Heidi back to the large pen they'd made for her.

Avery slipped from under Gator's arm. "I'm going to open the gate and see if she needs a hand."

"Be careful, babe," Gator said, with creases showing between his eyes.

Ellie cautioned the boys to move slowly, and they walked down as well, leaving Fink with Gator and McKoy.

"I hope you fellows don't mind, but I have some teacher assessments I need to fill out." He shook his head. "It's that time of year. Finally." He gave a scholarly grin and headed up to the house.

"Can't believe you're not running down there to help her." Gator had an innocent look on his face that didn't fool his best friend for a second.

"What are you driving at?"

"Just heard through the grapevine that you helped her build that nice, solid-looking fence. Figured you weren't doing it for your health."

"It's my job."

Gator snorted. "Forget who you're talking to?" He put his hand on the fence. "You're the animal control officer. Not the town fence builder."

McKoy didn't say anything. Gator was right. McKoy helped people all the time. But he'd never built a fence for anyone. He hated to admit it, but Jillian moved him in ways he'd never felt.

Gator's voice lowered. "I'm not knocking it, man. She's a nice girl. The whole time my mom was sick, Jillian helped Avery make meals and cheer her up. She's great with Fink and Ellie's boys and you'd be hard pressed to find a nicer person. You made a good choice." His elbow poked McKoy's arm that rested on the top rail of the fence.

"I can't force her to want me."

"I saw the expression on her face when you pulled in. I'd say she wants you, all right."

McKoy didn't know what Gator was talking about, but it warmed his insides to hear him say so.

"I think she has some things she doesn't want me to know." He knew she did. But he didn't want to seem like he was telling on her. Or digging for info.

Gator shrugged. "She can like you without trusting you. Once she feels like she can trust you with what's in her heart, then you'll find out." He grinned at McKoy. "You can't glower at her like that. Maybe that works for bears and stuff, but women are different."

"Oh, wow. He's been married for ten days and all of a sudden he's the woman expert." McKoy rolled his eyes.

"Avery seems to feel okay about me." At that moment, Avery came out from under the barn and started walking toward them. Gator's eyes hooked on her and he watched her like she was the best thing that ever happened to him. Which was probably true.

Avery gave Gator a sweet smile before turning to McKoy. "Nice fence you built. Jillian's pretty happy about it. Fink and Ellie are too, actually. I think they think it will keep their kids out."

"It should."

Avery gave him an assessing look with a half-smile. "Jillian always insisted that the dog-control guy was up to no good, but I think—" Her smile got bigger. "I think she's changed her opinion."

McKoy wasn't sure what that meant, but he hoped it was a good thing for him. He wasn't the most exciting thing to ever happen to anyone, and he wasn't totally convinced that he had what it took to keep a woman beside him, but his heart seemed to feel that Jillian was worth the risk.

His brain said after the excitement of travelling for the circus and the adventurous life she'd led that she'd never be happy staying in one spot in Pennsylvania.

That argument made a lot of sense. Unfortunately.

But the pull of his heart was strong.

It wasn't long before Ellie came out with the boys wrestling beside her. McKoy smiled at their antics. It wasn't that long ago that he'd been that young, trying to wrestle his sisters, who weren't the slightest bit interested in getting taken down by their little brother.

Suddenly, the image of a little dark-haired, black-eyed girl with his chin popped into his brain. Wow. He must really have it bad if he were imagining his and Jillian's children. He shook his head to get rid of the image. Dumb.

Ellie walked up to them with a pleasant look on her face. "Jillian said if you wanted to do your inspection, she was cleaning the pen."

McKoy nodded. He was so busy thinking about kids for the first time in his life, he'd forgotten why he was even here.

"Thanks, Miss Ellie. I'll go do that." He could have been down there fifteen minutes ago.

Gator snorted as he left, but he ignored his friend. He wasn't acting completely normal, and it was because of Jillian and how he felt about her. She felt something for him too, he just wasn't sure what.

"Hey," he said as he entered the darker area under the barn. He didn't want to startle her.

"Back here," she said.

"That was pretty impressive." He figured she'd know he was talking about her performance on Heidi.

"That was just a little of the stuff we did together. I had a whole act I did with Heidi and Hazel. There wasn't much solo stuff." She stroked down Heidi's leg. "But Heidi remembered everything perfectly."

"You looked good." He'd never been great with words, and now, when there was so much more in his heart than "you looked good," he couldn't get the words to come to his lips.

She dumped a shovelful of manure in the wheelbarrow. "Thanks."

The contradiction drew him. Beautiful performer. Talented animal trainer. Common laborer who wasn't too good to shovel poop.

But he couldn't stand around while she worked. "Here." He put his hand out for the shovel. "Let me do that."

He didn't give her a chance to disagree, but took the shovel and scooped up the big piles. She had produced what looked like a scrub brush and was brushing Heidi down. Heidi seemed to enjoy it—she stood completely still with her eyes closed.

He finished getting all the big piles and took the wheelbarrow out to dump it. When he came back she had put the brush away.

"I'm finished, unless you need more time?" Her voice was low and husky, like she hadn't used it in a while. Or maybe the same emotions he felt were closing her throat.

"I'm done. You're doing a perfect job with her. There's nothing to complain about."

They stood, just a few feet apart, facing each other. An uncomfortable silence fell between them as neither said anything nor moved to go.

Finally, she said, "How's Uncle Roy? I haven't been out this week yet."

"He's fine. I'm leaving tonight so I can be up north first thing in the morning."

"I'll make sure to take a run tomorrow, then," she said.

"I appreciate it." He shoved a hand in his pocket. "I'm not any closer to convincing him to move to a retirement community this week than I was last."

"He's probably afraid no one will come visit him if he does that." She pushed a hair back away from her face.

"Some of them aren't that far. I'd drive you there for the occasional visit."

"Well..."

Little pricks of shock ran up his neck, and his palms started to sweat.

She looked at the ground. "I finally talked to the man from Brazil who bought Hazel, Heidi's sister. His name's Mario."

He didn't say anything but wished they weren't under the barn. The light was dim and he couldn't quite read the expression in her eyes, as she avoided looking at him.

"He offered me a job taking care of Hazel. He's considering buying Heidi as well."

Heat flashed up his neck and his chest felt like it was going to explode. "You can't just move to Brazil because some stranger offered you a job." There was anger in his voice, but he hadn't raised it.

She was seriously thinking about moving to Brazil to work for a stranger? A rich stranger if he were buying and shipping elephants.

"I've talked to several people who know him. They say he's a decent fellow and treats his animals well."

"He offered you a job out of the blue?" Didn't she see how weird that was?

"He saw some pictures and videos of me. He's also talked to people who know me."

A muscle ticked in his cheek. His words came out tight. His heart hurt. "You're actually considering moving to Brazil?"

She shrugged. "I like adventure. I've always been on the move. And it's not like I don't know the language. They speak Portuguese, I think, but that won't be hard to pick up since I'm fluent in Spanish."

The back of his throat burned, and his lungs pulled deep breaths in and out. He couldn't stay. She already knew how he felt and she'd rejected him. He didn't need to stick around for more.

"Maybe that's for the best." He pulled his hand out of his pocket and turned to go. "I wasn't sure how all the complaints we've had here, with the kid getting bitten and everything, would look on the application process anyway. I was expecting to get a call. I could probably explain it all away—"

"I haven't started the application process."

He jerked around. "What?"

She squared her shoulders and looked him in the eye. "I haven't started the application process."

He clenched his jaw so tight his teeth squeaked. Red spots flashed in front of his eyes.

He wanted, no needed, to know why. She knew he was sticking his neck out for her. Why hadn't she started applying for the permit?

His phone buzzed. He almost ignored it, but he was on call this week. He didn't move his eyes from hers until his phone was out in his hand. Then he looked down. Louie's number.

With his lips pressed tight together, he gave her one last look before swiping his phone and striding away.

The next morning Jillian's feet pounded on the pavement. She was much earlier than she normally was—hopefully Uncle Roy was out of bed. It was barely light, but she couldn't sleep. How could she not think about McKoy?

It wasn't the anger on his face that bothered her. He had every right to be angry, and she expected it. The betrayal she'd seen there bothered her, of course.

He'd trusted her. And she let him down.

But the thing that really upset her, kept her from sleeping, was the next emotion that had swept the anger and betrayal away. Acceptance.

Like what she'd done to him was exactly what he'd expected.

She hated that. Apparently she wasn't the first woman who had betrayed him. Or maybe she'd just made him feel that he wasn't enough.

And he took it. Like he knew it.

He didn't understand, because he didn't know.

She couldn't stand that look on his face and knew the next time she saw him she'd have to tell him. As much as she didn't want him disappointed or angry at her, it was better than him thinking there was something wrong with him.

Uncle Roy was not out with his dogs when Jillian reached his house, so she paced his sidewalk for a minute or two until her breathing was under control and she could talk without panting. She walked up the steps and Uncle Roy opened the door before she could knock.

"Hey, Twisty. You're early. Just in time for breakfast. Come on in." He had a big smile on his face and held the door open wide.

Usually the dogs were yapping and jumping around his legs, but they weren't anywhere in sight.

"Where are Chatty and Bubbles?" she asked as she stepped in.

"The boy has 'em outside. Likes to watch the sunrise." Uncle Roy shuffled to the kitchen and Jillian followed. His paper lay spread out on the table and the smell of fresh coffee permeated the air.

"McKoy is here?" she asked incredulously. He'd said he was leaving last night. She hoped nothing had happened.

"Yeah. Just got back in a bit ago. Guess he took a shower and is going to bed for a while." He put a hand on the fridge handle. "I'll cook you some eggs and bacon."

"No, thanks. If you don't mind, I'm going to go talk to McKoy for a minute."

"Don't mind at all. Take your time. I want to finish reading the paper and I haven't even started the crossword yet."

She walked over and put her hand on the back door knob. Through the window she could see McKoy, wearing only a pair of athletic shorts, standing with a steaming mug of coffee in hand, a bare shoulder propped against the porch post as he stared off at the orange- and pink-tinted sky. The dogs frolicked in the far corner of the big, fenced yard.

She paused for a moment, letting her eyes drift over the muscle ridges in his back as he took a sip of coffee and set his cup on the banister, before she opened the door softly.

"Hey, Uncle Roy," he said without turning around.

She didn't answer, but closed the door behind her. Uncle Roy sat around the side of the table, and she couldn't see him once the door was closed.

Moving forward she feathered a touch on his shoulder.

His head jerked around, his brows smashed together between his eyes. Eyes that opened wide when he saw her. He froze.

Her fingers stayed where they were, the skin of his shoulder hot and smooth under them.

He'd said she could touch his shoulders anytime. She could see the promise reflected in his eyes. It didn't matter that he was angry with her. That she'd betrayed his trust and deceived him into thinking she was applying for a permit she had no intention of getting.

He'd made a promise and he was keeping it.

She'd known he would. But she wanted him to know she knew.

The anger that had flared in his eyes when he'd seen her banked some, like her touch soothed it.

She swallowed hard and took a breath. "I didn't apply for the permit, because I knew they wouldn't give it to me."

His eyes narrowed. "Yes they would. You're the perfect candidate. You have experience with elephants, which is a requirement. Your enclosure is more than adequate. I know the money could be an issue, but we can figure something out."

Her hand moved off his shoulder and touched his lips.

It wasn't anger that flared in his eyes, then.

Her heart stampeded and electric shocks tripped through her veins at the heat in his eyes. She could feel the answering flames in her own body.

His hands settled on her hips, and she doubted he even realized they were there. He was too busy searching her eyes, her face, trying to find the answer to the question he thought was unanswerable.

Her hands moved to his bare shoulders and she stepped closer. His looked became fiercer, but his brows still puckered, like he was trying to figure out if she truly meant what her body language was saying.

She spared him the contemplation by standing on tiptoe, lifting her head and pressing her lips to his. Warm and firm, they were everything she'd thought they might be, and more.

A rumble came from his throat, and his hands tightened on her hips before they slid around her back, pulling her toward him. The full body contact shocked her senses, and she gasped, breaking their lips apart.

Their breath mingled as they stared at each other, chests heaving, hearts thumping. His pulse jumped erratically in his throat.

Her knees trembled.

Her hands burned where they touched his hot skin, and his fingers sent a stream of sensation through her body from where they held her back as gently as he might cradle a baby.

"Jillian," he whispered. "Kiss me again."

Her body moved closer automatically, even as her mind screamed no.

She stopped, a heartbeat away from his lips. "I'm illegal."

That wrinkle appeared in his brows again. "To me? You're illegal to me?" His voice held confusion, but he didn't pull away. His hands still held her, his body still leaned toward her. His lips almost brushed hers.

She didn't want to go on, didn't want to ruin what she had, standing in his arms. But she opened her mouth and forced the words out. "No. I paid to take a tunnel under the Rio Grande and spent five days in the desert." The whole group of them had almost died. "I can't get a permit for Heidi, because I'm not a citizen. I'm not a legal resident. Not even close."

He didn't move as he processed what she'd just said. She could see as understanding started to dawn across his face. The line between his brows disappeared. His eyes widened before his brows lowered.

Anger.

Yes, that's what she expected. "The papers I showed you for Heidi were forged. I don't have legal papers for her, either."

His eyes widened and a vein stood out on his forehead.

Still, he didn't move. Didn't let go of her. Didn't push her away.

A small shoot of hope started to bud in her chest. She slid both hands to his shoulders and stared into his eyes.

The remembrance of his promise flashed, conflicting with his new knowledge of her. What she'd done. What she was.

"Ah, Jillian." Her name ripped from his throat. He leaned his head back, closing his eyes against the struggle that was happening in his head.

Her fingers dug into his shoulders and her chest burned. She should never have put him in this position. He followed the rules. He *enforced* the rules. How could she ask him to break them for her?

Being with her wasn't necessarily breaking the rules, but it was stretching the limits of what his conscience would allow. He wasn't faking the struggle that raged over his face, nor the tension in his muscles under her fingers.

Which cut straight to her heart. How could she make him choose?

She couldn't.

Her hands dropped and she backed away. His fingers flexed before relaxing and allowing her to slide out of his embrace.

His jaw bunched, and his eyes, half-open, filled with betrayal and longing, followed her movements. But he didn't speak.

She could hardly stand his silence. Worse than if he'd ranted at the top of his lungs. Anger, she could deal with.

The pain in his eyes? No.

Chapter 13

M cKoy got dressed and went in to work. He wasn't going to sleep anyway, might as well be productive somewhere.

He couldn't stop thinking about Jillian. When she said "illegal" she'd meant herself. *She* was here, in the US, illegally.

He enforced the law. Sure, his area of authority didn't extend to what she was doing wrong, but the whole idea went against his personal code of honor.

There were a ton of rules that he didn't like, yet every single day he enforced them. Some of them didn't make any sense. Why did a person have to be a citizen to have a permit to house an elephant anyway? What did it matter? But a rule was a rule. You couldn't break them just because you didn't agree with them.

He knew that.

He believed that.

He lived that.

Except now he was torn. Did knowing that Jillian wasn't here legally make him complicit in her crime? Or, maybe more accurately, did Jillian breaking the law to be here make him want to be with her less? Was there something wrong with him because he didn't care?

He couldn't believe that he'd gotten to that point—that he didn't care that every day she was breaking the law of the country he loved, just to be here. He hadn't known that his feelings were growing that strong.

But he wasn't a slave to his feelings. Never had been. He had never allowed himself to be ruled by how he felt. He'd lived by an outside moral code that didn't change according to his inside, volatile feelings. Sure, it was a harder way to live, but even now, when his heart begged him to do something different, he knew it was the right way.

But the right action? He wasn't sure.

He was also bound by his word. He'd told her she could touch him anytime. She'd tested that today. And she knew his struggle. Maybe that was why she'd walked away.

He also couldn't say for sure that if he'd been born in Mexico that he wouldn't be trying as hard as he could to get into the US.

Actually, no. He knew he wouldn't. He'd be trying as hard as he could to make his birth country a better place. But maybe that was a product of where he'd been born and raised. He'd be a completely different person if he'd been born in Mexico.

All these thoughts, plus his jumbled-up feelings of want and desire for Jillian, were zapping through his body, so he wasn't prepared for the shock he got when he walked in the office.

Loretta motioned him back to Louie's office. "Just go in," she said.

He'd texted Louie, so his boss knew he was coming.

"Hey, come on in," Louie said as McKoy pushed the door open. Somehow he'd known Todd would be in there, too. He walked in, feeling weary and heavy, like his skin was made out of lead.

"We have a solution to the elephant problem." Louie glanced at Todd, who sat in the chair in front of the desk with a big smirk on his face.

McKoy had thought he'd been through all the emotion he could handle for one day, but anxiety cramped his stomach. Whatever was going to be said next would affect Jillian. He needed to protect her. Whatever the confusion surrounding his feelings for her, he knew that much.

"Todd has found a buyer at a zoo out west. Their last elephant died of old age, and they want this one." Louie watched McKoy carefully. "I've also decided to relieve you of the elephant inspec-tion duty. I think Todd's right and you're a little too emotionally involved, plus you're on that cock-fighting ring that you were called out for last night. I want to see that report, by the way. But in the meantime I'm giving the elephant case to Todd."

Todd shrugged like it wasn't a big deal. "We already have several complaints. If she's out of compliance even once, we can confiscate the animal and sell it to the zoo. You know what an elephant sells for?" Todd's brows lifted, indicating it was a huge sum of money.

"You can't make things up." McKoy's voice was devoid of the emotions that wanted to erupt out of his chest.

"I won't need to." They both knew there were so many regulations that it was almost impossible to follow every single one. Normally, they'd give a verbal warning and give an owner time to fix any problems, even though they weren't required to by law.

"There isn't a thing out of place in her boarding kennel or in the elephant pen." He couldn't protest being taken off Jillian's case. There was no way he could argue that he wasn't emotionally involved. But if Todd was going to go in there and take Heidi over some obscure infraction, it wasn't right and everyone in the room knew it.

"The case is out of your hands," Louie said. "Let it go." His eyes said if McKoy couldn't allow this to fade out, it would only prove what Todd had been arguing all along—that McKoy was too emotionally involved to have been doing a good job on the case.

"Is that all you wanted?" McKoy asked.

"Yes."

"I'll go get that report from last night written." He turned and left, closing the door carefully behind him when what he really wanted to do was slam it. It didn't bode well for his chances of getting the promotion if he was being removed from a case and Todd was being reassigned. That almost never happened.

It would hit him soon, he was sure, but currently he didn't really care if he got the promotion or not. Everything he believed had been called into question, and he wasn't sure where to turn to figure out where he was.

By lunch the report was finished. He turned it in before leaving for the day. His first thought was that he'd go out to Jillian's, but he no longer had a reason to.

He needed to warn her about Todd, but Todd was headed out east for the rest of the week, so he wouldn't be making a visit to Jillian until at least Monday, unless he made an exception to his no working on weekends rule. But McKoy couldn't imagine that things had changed that much, so he had a few days anyway.

He went home.

Uncle Roy was sitting on the front porch. Despite the overcast skies, the day was warm, and the old man rocked slowly in his rocking chair. Chatty was in his lap, and Bubbles lay at his feet. They didn't stir when McKoy trudged up the stairs, so he guessed they'd spent the morning practicing the tricks that Jillian was teaching them and running around.

Bone weary after being up all night with the cock-fighting ring lead, he would just toss and turn if he tried to go to sleep, so he slumped against the post and slid down until he sat on the edge of the steps, one leg bent in front of him, one braced on the second step.

"Rough day?" Uncle Roy asked.

"And it's only half over. Looks like yours was exciting. Dogs are spent, anyway."

"Yep. Been working on the things that Twisty's taught us." Uncle Roy flashed his dentures. "She's a good kid. Kinda seems like she likes you, too."

He smirked, and McKoy wondered if he'd seen their embrace this morning, if not the kiss, which had been entirely too short as far as he was concerned. Too short, but the best kiss he'd ever had.

"Both of you'ins seemed upset when you left this morning."

"Yeah."

Uncle Roy rocked in silence for a while. Finally he shifted, patting the head of the dog on his lap. "You want to talk about it?

"I can't, really." But he could. Uncle Roy wouldn't tell anyone. He studied the hand that hung over his knee. "She's not an American citizen."

"So?" Uncle Roy asked.

Uncle Roy didn't understand.

"She's not here legally."

"Oh." He rubbed the dog's head absently, his rocking chair keeping its slow rhythm.

McKoy ran a hand over his head, then looked out over the greening grass. After his fiancée told him he was boring, he'd figured that was the end for him. It was easy to see she was right. He wasn't a big party guy. He didn't find flaunting authority exciting or interesting, and he'd just as soon stay home as go out. Girls wouldn't find him interesting, and that was fine. But he couldn't deny he'd wanted someone to share things with. To be with him. To love him.

Someone to work alongside of him. Someone to talk to. Someone he could look at and admire, who he could run his eyes over their body and know it was his to touch at any time. Someone who would touch him.

He closed his eyes. The need for Jillian to touch him made his skin prick. He hadn't realized how much he'd longed for that human contact. Not just any human. He wanted Jillian's hands. Her lips. Her body touching his.

Her smile in the morning. Her laughter all day long.

Ugh. He had to quit torturing himself.

"So marry her."

"Huh?" McKoy said, jerking out of his thoughts. Marry her?

"Marry her."

"Does that automatically make her legal?" He couldn't believe it would be that easy. "How could I, anyway? Don't you need your birth certificate?" He rubbed his neck. He hadn't been thinking about marriage. He wasn't even sure Jillian liked him that much. But maybe it was a possibility. A far distant one.

"I don't know. Guys who were in the service with me did it—married girls they met overseas and brought them home as their wife."

"I guess I'd have to ask a lawyer about it. That sounds too simple." McKoy leaned his head back against the post and closed his eyes. Marriage was out of the question. He couldn't believe he was even thinking of going to a lawyer's.

Although...if he had a bit of time, marriage might not be so bad. Except, he didn't really want Jillian marrying him so she could become a citizen. Especially if she didn't really like him and considered him boring.

By Sunday night, McKoy knew he'd put off telling Jillian long enough. He hadn't seen her since she kissed him, then left. Not that he'd expected her to look him up. It was probably his responsibility to make the next move in their relationship. Did they have a relationship?

He wasn't sure.

In his book they did. That kiss made it a relationship. That wasn't something he went around doing with just anyone. Jillian was special. Special in herself. Special to him.

But he couldn't deny he was leery. He wasn't any more interesting now than he was, and although he'd chatted with a lawyer over the phone and marrying someone who wasn't a US citizen was a little more complicated than it sounded, it could be done, although probably not in time to get her a permit for Heidi. But he didn't want her marrying him just to gain citizenship status.

But if he cared for her, should it matter whether she used him or not? Shouldn't he be willing to sacrifice for her, even if his feelings weren't returned? Or were his feelings contingent on hers?

Navigating the tricky world of feelings was a lot harder than seeing the solid black lines of rules and following them.

He drove his truck slowly down the drive toward her house, his hands sweating on the steering wheel.

He wasn't great at taking risks, and seeing Jillian today felt like a risk.

Getting her number from Fink or Gator had been something he'd considered. But that felt like the easy way out. He needed to face her.

Four days had been long enough without seeing her.

She was sitting on her porch step, Snickers at her feet. His eyes roamed over her as he drove the last distance and parked.

She wore jeans that stopped mid-calf and a flowy, peasant-type white blouse, which emphasized her dark skin and contrasted with her black hair that fell in a shiny waterfall over her shoulder. The neck on the blouse was big and fell over, exposing one bare shoulder. His eyes traced the smooth curve of her skin. It would taste like honey and spices, he was sure of it.

He sat for a moment in his pickup, gripping the wheel. He couldn't think about tasting her skin. Or even touching it. He had things to tell her and he needed to focus on giving information.

But as he looked at her, sitting there with her hand on her dog, he couldn't help but remember her determination to work with blistered hands. Her care for her animals. How she burnt their food.

That last thought made him smile, and he got out of his pickup. He walked to the front of it and leaned against the grill, leaving a good ten feet between them.

"You have a minute?" he asked.

She tilted her head, looking at him like she'd expected something more.

They weren't exactly on terms where he would greet her with a kiss, were they?

"Yes," she said softly, her hand moving on Snicker's fur.

"My boss took me off your case."

She snorted a quick laugh without humor. "You told him that we kissed?"

He searched her face. He couldn't tell if the idea that he might have been honest bothered her or not. He hoped it didn't.

"No."

Her black eyes snapped to his.

"That's not something I'd go around telling people about." Even if it was the thing he'd most thought about. All week. More. He wanted more.

He shoved his hands in his pockets. "Todd found a circus who will buy your elephant. That impressed Louie."

"That might be a good thing." Her eyes looked straight ahead, staring at nothing while she rolled that over in her head.

"Could be. Although, sounded to me like Todd was going to find some infraction against you, take the elephant, and then sell it himself, getting the money for our department, which is constantly underfunded." It was a pet peeve of his that Philly got the lion's share of Pennsylvania's tax money. The little that was spared for animal control was spread thin.

Jillian continued to stare out across the field. "I'm not looking to get money out of her. But that would mean she'd never be reunited with her sister."

"You hear from the man who has her?" He didn't want to ask, but he needed to.

"Yes." Her chin tilted up and she looked square at him. "He'll take her if I go with her."

His body froze, and the world seemed to stop around him. Their eyes clashed. Hers defiant, and his, heck, he didn't know what his might look like.

Devastated, maybe.

Desperate, probably.

Pleading, most definitely.

She couldn't kiss him with such power and emotion then move eight thousand miles away.

Oh, yes she could. He had no claim on her at all.

"Walk with me?" he asked softly.

She swallowed and looked down.

He thought she was going to refuse. But then she stood, gracefully, straightening.

Pulling his hands out of his pockets, he pushed off from the grill of his truck. "I always feel like such a clod beside you."

Her brows tilted down. "Why?"

"Because you move with such elegance and grace." His heart hammered, but he let the words in his heart slip off his tongue. "I could watch you all day long and never get tired of your beauty and poise."

"I see that you watch me."

"I can't not watch you."

She'd stopped in front of him. His mind and heart waged a short battle. His heart won, because he reached out and took her hand, watching her face, hoping that was acceptance in her eyes.

His rough hand slid over her lissome fingers, sweet and sensuous as they bent and curved together.

Her chest moved as she took a shaky breath. "We can walk around the pond. It's pretty in the moonlight and the peepers are singing."

He could hear them now that she mentioned it. Could hear the breeze rustle the pines, which scented the air with their fragrance.

"I'll follow." He wasn't a very good follower. Never had been. But Jillian seemed to carry his heart.

"I wasn't sure I'd see you again," she said as she stepped out. Her body flowed easily beside his.

"Why?" He couldn't imagine not seeing her again.

"I felt like you'd never talk to me again once you realized I snuck in." Her head stayed straight ahead, like she was afraid to look at him. Or maybe she was just trying to make sure of where she was going as the sun disappeared behind the mountain. "I know I put you in a bad spot."

He heard her, but he didn't really want to talk about that. He was more concerned about whether or not she was actually going to move to Brazil. Would this night be their last night together?

She seemed to be waiting for him to say something, though. He didn't want to tell her of his struggle. How he wanted to follow the law but, for the first time in his life, was thinking about letting his emotions rule his decision. Not completely. He'd talked to that lawyer.

"I realized I didn't care." He'd come to the conclusion that being here unlawfully was wrong. But he didn't think that Jillian was normally a lawbreaker. He couldn't feel for her so deeply if he believed that about her.

"Really?" Surprise laced her tone. "I can't believe that."

"Maybe it's not entirely true. I do care. But only because of the hurdles it places between me and you."

Her eyes widened.

He'd said, twice now, things that allowed her to glimpse what he was feeling for her. But she hadn't responded in kind. He wasn't going to wait around. If she were thinking of going to Brazil, he didn't have time to be slow.

He waited until they stopped a few yards away from the pond. He turned her to face him. "Is there a you and me, Jillian?"

"Do you want there to be?"

"That wasn't what I asked."

"You haven't talked to me for four days."

"I left the next day and was up north until Friday." It wasn't an excuse, and he knew it.

She didn't even call him on it. Instead, she prompted, "Yesterday?"

"It took me that long to figure out what I could live with." It was a bad choice of words and he knew it as soon as they came out of his mouth. Her face scrunched up, and she turned away.

"I don't want to be someone you have to convince yourself you can 'live with.'" She wrapped her arms around her body and stared out at the pond.

He didn't know how to get himself out of that hole, so he asked something safer. "Tell me about your childhood."

"I grew up in the circus." She shrugged, like it was no big deal. Maybe it wasn't to her, since it was her "normal." "It was just my mom and me. She's still in Mexico, married with young kids. I guess she was just a kid herself when she had me, but it didn't seem like that growing up."

He wanted to touch her, to put his arm around her, but there was something else he felt he needed to ask first. "Is there anything else that maybe someone who was too stupid to talk to you for four days after you kissed him might need to know before he grovels and apologizes and begs you to kiss him again?"

She smiled, and his heart did a small flip. "I have a lot of secrets, McKoy."

"I'm sorry I didn't try to talk to you before this. I could have gotten your number. I could have come yesterday. Even Friday night, it wasn't that late when I got home." He balled his hands into fists so he wouldn't trace the curve of her neck, the edge of her blouse, thread his fingers through her hair. "You're all I thought about for the last four days. I longed with every breath I took to see you again. But I didn't know, I still don't, if there's any future for us."

"Does it matter?" she asked softly. The breeze lifted strands of her hair and blew them across her face. She turned back to him.

It did. Of course it mattered. He wasn't the kind of guy who just…just what? Had a fling? Played the field? God forbid, a one-night stand?

No way. He didn't operate like that. Never had. Maybe that made him boring. He didn't care.

"Yes." His voice was low but fierce. "Yes, it matters. I don't go around kissing whatever girl strikes my fancy. Or whatever girl will let me, or however guys do those things." He closed the distance between them. "I don't live to gratify myself today and have no regard for tomorrow and its consequences. A casual indifference to the person I'm with. Indulge and move on? No."

She blinked at him like he'd just sprouted a second head. "You don't date?"

That question totally took the wind out of his sails and he turned away, stuffing his hands in his pockets. "I was engaged once. Back when I was in college. We were pretty serious and making plans. But she went to study in Europe for a year. She left my ring there and brought a guy back with her."

He turned and met her eyes. "She told me I was predictable and boring. That and the fact that she obviously cheated on me made me decide it was better to be alone."

"You're not boring."

Words he wanted to hear. Maybe needed to hear.

"Actually, I think she was right. I enjoy having guidelines written down. Something I can see so I know where the boundary is. That's boring."

"That's hard. To live in bounds." She gave a humorless laugh.

He thought of the boundary she had crossed—a country's boundary.

"I might have a solution to your problem."

"Oh?"

"Marry me."

Chapter 14

J illian gasped. He wanted her to marry him?

Her heart stilled. He hadn't asked, and it wasn't romantic. He presented it as a solution to her problem. All the compassion in her chest that had built up from hearing what his fiancée had done to him drained out of her.

She had longed to put her arms around him and kiss him again. A longer, deeper kiss. Would it be as sweet as the one they'd shared earlier this week? As powerful? As life-changing?

It had haunted her for the last four days, but he'd not called. She could only assume it hadn't meant to him what it meant to her. Or maybe the better assumption was that he couldn't deal with the things she'd told him.

Oh, but there was more.

"You know, you don't get to use those tunnels for free."

Lines appeared between his brows.

"They're there for drugs. Smugglers deal in people, too, but people are much bigger, harder to hide, and less profitable. Why risk having border patrol find your lucrative tunnel? It needs to be worthwhile for them, so they charge us. A lot."

"I ask you to marry me and I get a lecture on how to use a drug cartel tunnel to illegally cross into America?" There was irritation, but also humor, in his voice.

She smiled. Everything didn't have to be so serious. "No. You asked about my secrets. I'm telling you. I owe a drug runner a lot of money. Thousands. I also owe the person who drove me from Arizona to here several thousand dollars."

"A bus ticket would have been cheaper."

"I know that now, but I didn't at the time. Chalk that up to Mexicans taking advantage of Mexicans."

"Sad."

"They prey on the stupidity and fear of new arrivals. Of course, there is some risk for them, as well. You probably can't claim innocence if you're caught with a carful of undocumented humans." She lifted her shoulder. She couldn't solve her country's problems by herself.

"Problems that need to be solved. But not tonight."

She moved closer to him. "No. No problem solving tonight."

He eyed her like she might bite him. She almost laughed. What was he afraid she might do?

He took a small step back, then seemed to brace himself as she followed, keeping just an inch of space between them.

"I still don't understand," he said. "Why did I need to know that, tonight?"

"Because you asked." She touched his shoulder. His eyes flared and his breath hissed. He knew exactly what she was doing and he stood for it, maybe even leaned closer.

"Jillian," he said, warning clear in his tone.

"You asked what you need to know before you grovel and ask me to kiss you again. That's it."

His whole body seemed to immobilize with shock. She could feel it radiating off him in waves.

Maybe it was no wonder, since he'd demanded she marry him, and she'd responded with a lecture on drug cartels and a no-strings plea to kiss her. Probably not the response he was looking for. Although what, exactly, he'd thought she'd do when he demanded she marry him to solve her problems, like taking a pill to get rid of a fever, she had no idea.

"I'm sorry," he said. "That moment when your lips touched mine was the most amazing moment of my life, and I've done nothing but think about it every second since. I wanted to follow you out the door. I wanted to be with you. I picked up my phone a hundred times and even called Gator twice, but never asked for your number. I didn't want to pursue something that had no meaning, no matter how badly I wanted it. I had to decide, first, that it didn't matter. I'm sorry. Please forgive me." His voice dropped low. "Please. Kiss me again. Let me hold you."

Any irritation she still felt disappeared with the knowledge of his struggle.

There had never been a reluctance to kiss him, but desire surged within her when he asked, begged, for her.

She stepped into him and moved her hands to his shoulders, their eyes meeting at the promise between them. Moving her hands around his neck she pressed into him and felt his body tremble at her touch.

His head lowered, but he whispered, "I want a commitment. I want a promise. Something that says you're not leaving me."

Her head moved slowly back and forth. "Just kiss me."

He let out a low groan before his lips touched hers. But she wasn't allowing butterfly touches that only made her dream about more. Tugging on his head, she deepened the kiss, and he went along. Eagerly.

The dusk seemed to close around them as her whole being focused on the man in front of her. Her heart kicked and knocked, and her lungs begged for air as the world spun and shifted, bursting into brilliant light behind her closed eyes.

She had no idea how long it was until he lifted his head, their lips still clinging, and sighed, resting his cheek on the top of her hair, pulling her body close to his.

Happy for his strength, for his strong arms around her, holding her, because her knees trembled, almost knocking together, she pressed her hot cheek against his chest and wrapped her arms around him.

"You amaze me," he whispered. His voice held a tremor, like he was still affected by their kiss.

"It's you," she said, her voice hoarse. "It's all you."

Monday morning, Todd arrived at Jillian's place to do an inspection. He nosed around the kennels until she set her shovel aside and led him out to the barn. Heidi seemed to go into a deeper depression every day, and she stood in a corner while Todd looked around.

"The place looks great. You're passing with flying colors." He turned around and, as though just making small talk, he asked. "How's the permit process coming?"

"Just fine, thank you." It was misleading, but there could hardly be anything wrong with a process she hadn't started.

"Glad to hear it. I'm going to write up a glowing report. That should help you." His lips turned up before he strutted away.

Jillian's distrust of government workers came back with more force than it had previously. She didn't trust him. But he had seemed so sincere. Did that make everything McKoy had told her wrong?

She didn't think so, but couldn't stop the question from forming in her brain. After he'd walked her back up to her porch, he'd given her his number.

Waiting until Todd's car pulled out of sight, she pulled it up and sent him a text.

Todd said I passed the inspection with flying colors.

It was a few minutes before he texted back. She assumed he probably wasn't standing around with his phone in his hand. Finally, it dinged.

That's good. I'll let you know if I hear anything.

He'd specifically told her that his phone was personal, although he did have a government issued one that he hardly ever used. She appreciated knowing it was okay to talk about personal things.

After jogging to Uncle Roy's and spending some time there, she went to the post office. Not wanting to be panting when she walked up the steps, she stopped around the corner of the building and put her hands on her knees, catching her breath.

Two men were engaged in a conversation just around the corner. That wouldn't have concerned her, but when she heard one of them say "elephant" her ears pricked up. Then she heard the word "bribe." Up until that point she hadn't been eavesdropping on purpose. But with those words buzzing in her ear, she straightened and flattened herself against the bricks, edging to the corner.

"They wired the money last week. They want to see something soon."

"I need a week." Todd's voice. She wouldn't have known it, except he'd been out at her place just an hour ago. "There's a conference in Somerset that I have to go to and I'm leaving right now. I'll be back Friday."

"Jillian?"

Jillian jerked her head around. Gail Patton, the nurse at the emergency clinic in town, and a single mother of a sweet little boy, looked at her with a tilted head. It was pretty much impossible to pretend she was doing anything normal, but the townspeople didn't expect her to be normal.

She moved back away from the edge and through the grass to the sidewalk, not wanting Todd to hear her voice. "I've always wondered if I could climb a building backwards." She shrugged and smiled. "Guess not."

Gail laughed, and Jillian remembered that she'd been one of the few, very few, who hadn't judged her harshly for being so different. "Bennett has heard in school that there's an elephant out at your place, and he's been begging, like on his knees, little-boy begging, for me to take him out to see it. I don't suppose?" She lifted her brows.

In a normal situation, Jillian might have said no, but everyone knew Gail's story of how some loser had sweet talked her, gotten her pregnant, and left her. Now she struggled to raise their child on her own.

So she agreed, suggesting they do it this Friday after school.

Todd and the man he was with were gone by the time she got done talking to Gail, and Jillian hurried up the stairs, trying to figure out if she should go to McKoy with her new, partial, knowledge.

Her brain whispered that she knew she couldn't trust government employees, while the rest of her said that McKoy would never lie to her. He was as straight as a ruler, and the most honorable man she knew.

So she texted him when she got home. He'd be driving to the same conference Todd was going to, so she wasn't surprised when he didn't text back.

Her phone ringing in her hand did startle her, though. "Hello," she said.

"Jillian, my darling. Have you made a decision?" It was Mario, from Brazil.

McKoy's kiss had tied her all up in knots and she didn't know what she wanted anymore. Although, she was sure she wanted Heidi to go to a good home. A zoo would probably be a good place, but she wasn't sure what the bribe was about.

"I'm not moving to Brazil." There. She said it.

"I'm sorry to hear that."

"But I would still like for you to take Heidi."

"I don't have anyone who can take care of her. And her sister is not doing well."

Jillian's breath caught. "What do you mean, not doing well?"

"She won't eat."

Not good. At this point, Jillian wasn't even sure that being reunited with her sister would help Hazel. And seeing Hazel die might kill

Heidi. Elephants felt a family member's death very deeply. Panic clawed its way up her spine.

"Are you sure she's not sick?"

"My veterinarian says not."

Then it must be loneliness or depression or both.

Suddenly, Mario said, "I need to go. Think about it, my dear. You'll need to make up your mind by this weekend."

He hung up and Jillian was left staring into space, wondering what in the world she was going to do. Could she save Hazel if she agreed to go down with Heidi?

She wasn't any closer to deciding that night when McKoy called.

"Hello?" She knew exactly who it was. She'd checked the caller ID. But they hadn't done much talking after he'd kissed her last night. He was leaving today, and she'd said she'd check on Uncle Roy, which she had, both in the morning and also in the late afternoon, but they'd not talked anymore about them.

Whatever "them" was.

"Hey."

It seemed like he might be at a loss for words. She wondered if it would have been different if she'd have said yes when he commanded her to marry him. Maybe.

"I haven't called Uncle Roy yet."

"Oh?" It made her feel good that she was his first call.

"They just let us out a bit ago, and I grabbed a bite before coming back to my room. Swanky hotel."

She laughed at the way he said "swanky." He wasn't a pretentious person, and anything better than a Motel 8 was probably high-class for him. For her, too. Although, there had been plenty of people in the circus who had led glamorous lives before landing there, and they loved to talk about them.

"You're alone?" she asked. Maybe not the most important question in the world, but the one that she most wanted to know.

"Yeah." Material crinkling came through the phone like he was lying down on the bed. It wasn't hard to picture him stretched out on the comforter, one hand behind his head, his biceps flexed. "Some of the guys were going out, but I wasn't interested."

Her heart dipped and twirled. But her brain shut it down. He wouldn't have been interested in going out with the guys even if it hadn't been for her.

"Actually, it was all I could do to wait to call you until I got back here. Pathetic, isn't it?"

"That makes me happy."

He chuckled. "How's Heidi?"

"She's sad. And Mario, that's the guy from Brazil, said that Hazel wasn't eating. I need to make a decision about what I'm doing. He's calling this weekend, and he'll want to know."

There was silence on the other end.

Their kiss rolled through her mind. It made her fingers tingle.

And the man was in his hotel room, talking on the phone with her rather than going out with everyone else. She could see some people calling that boring, but that was exactly the kind of man she wanted. Someone happy at home.

Finally, he spoke in a rough voice that was pitched real low. "If you need to go to Brazil, if you think that will save the elephants that you love, don't let me stop you."

"You're the only thing keeping me from going." She had to be honest with him. She could leave her dog kennels, and the business she had just started. As much as she didn't want to, she could. But there was no way in the world she would ever find a man as good as McKoy. And that he seemed to want her was amazing.

He was quiet for a while, and she almost said she was going to hang up, when he spoke again.

"I don't even have a passport."

"You would consider moving to Brazil?" Her voice squeaked, but she couldn't help it. Unbelievable.

"Crazy, isn't it?" He laughed, sounding a little self-derisive. "I was running it over in my head, trying to figure out how to make it work."

"You could." She could get excited about McKoy in Brazil.

"I think Gator and Avery would look after Uncle Roy, but I hate to leave him."

Her face fell, and she put her head in her hand. She'd forgotten about Uncle Roy. "What about your job?"

"I love it, but the travelling was getting harder with Uncle Roy and I wouldn't want to do that if..." His voice trailed off.

"If what?" she prompted him.

"I was going to say something presumptuous."

"Say it."

"If I had you."

She closed her eyes, unable to believe that he was thinking that way. Her body felt warm and happy.

"What would you do?"

"I don't know. I guess we'll see if I get the job."

There was rustling on the other end, and he said, "I'd better let you go. I know you have to start early tomorrow."

"Thanks for calling."

"My pleasure. Jillian?"

"Yeah?"

"I'll be home Friday afternoon. Would you like to do something Friday night?"

She jumped up, almost fist-pumping. "Like a date?" Her voice only sounded a little squeaky.

"Yeah."

"I'd love to." She noticed he didn't press her to give a commitment. Didn't even ask her to make a decision between him or going to Brazil. Actually, he was thinking of going with her is what it sounded like. If she hadn't been talking to him herself, she would hardly believe it.

"I'll look forward to it," he said. "Maybe I'll give you a call tomorrow night?"

"Sounds great." She jumped up and down as they hung up, then couldn't control herself any longer and did backbends down the steps and off the porch.

She fell asleep with a smile on her face.

Chapter 15

I 'm with Uncle Roy in the ER. He was on the ground this morning when I came over. Said he had a dizzy spell and fell down.

The message was on McKoy's phone when he walked out of the bathroom after taking a shower the next morning.

I'll be there in two. He typed quickly and hurriedly got dressed, throwing his stuff in his bags.

It was a little under two hours later that he was texting Jillian, asking where they were. He'd taken care of things with Louie, but if he was running neck and neck with Todd for the promotion, he'd probably just lost it, even though this shouldn't count against him.

The ER beds were separated by curtains, and he was counting up to the third one where Jillian said they were when her head popped out.

Her eyes showed worry, but also a little uncertainty, as though their conversation last night when he'd mentioned wanting to be with her, and having her be his and the crazy idea he'd had of going to Brazil, of all places, to be with her, had thrown her off.

He had no idea why his lips had gotten so loose, but he did know his feelings for Jillian had only gotten stronger. He'd never felt anything like this in his life, and he didn't want to lose someone as amazing as she was without having a chance to be with her.

Casual and temporary weren't things he'd ever considered doing in relationships, and here he was, possibly doing both.

But he wouldn't push her.

"Hey." He figured if she didn't like the way he'd greeted her, she needed to say something. Reaching her, he wrapped his arms around her and breathed in her cotton-candy scent.

She didn't hesitate, but wrapped her arms around him, pressing herself to him and holding on tight.

"I was so scared," she mumbled against his shirt.

"You called the ambulance and got him here. It's going to be okay."

"He was on the floor and I thought he was dead at first."

His hands rubbed lightly up and down her back. "It sounded like he was doing good."

"Yeah." She pulled him back behind the curtain. Uncle Roy wasn't there.

"They took him for tests to be sure, but the doctor is saying his blood sugar was low and he might have just had a dizzy spell."

"I see." McKoy nodded. She moved back into his arms and he held her close, loving the feel of her in his arms.

"I'm so glad you're here. I'm never good in hospitals," she whispered.

"We'll just deal with what comes, when it comes." He held her head against his chest. "Do you need a drink or anything?"

"No. Thank you. Maybe you didn't have breakfast?"

"I didn't, but I think I'll wait."

"I think I ought to go home and take care of the dogs. I'm not sure they got out this morning." Her arms didn't loosen from around him. Made him feel good.

"If you don't mind, I should call the family and let them know in case any of them want to come." He doubted his sisters would. And his dad probably wouldn't make the trip up from Florida for a dizzy spell. Not unless there was something else found.

"Ellie said she was running some errands so she could pick me up and drop me off."

He hated to have her leave, but the dogs did need to be cared for.

Once Jillian had left with Ellie, he settled in the chair and called his dad, who said exactly what McKoy had thought he would—that he'd wait and see if it was something serious.

He fingered his phone, considering whether he could get away with not calling his sisters. He figured they wouldn't want to come, but they might get angry if he didn't call. Finally, he bit the bullet and called Tara. Pam was the oldest and the most likely to tell him he was doing everything wrong. He saved her for last.

Tara was easy. She didn't answer so he left a message.

Pam answered on the first ring. "McKoy. What's the problem?"

"I'm in the ER with Uncle Roy. He had a dizzy spell and fell down. They're running tests now. Just wanted to let you know." There. He got it all out in one breath.

"What do you think the problem is?"

"The doctor suggested low blood sugar. I haven't seen him. My...girlfriend found him this morning when she came to check on him."

"Where were you?"

"At a work conference."

"Hmm. I see. Well you should get the house out of his name as soon as you can. If he has to go to an old folks' home, we won't get squat out of the inheritance." Pam sounded put out, but businesslike.

McKoy was pretty sure she didn't mean that quite the way it sounded, but his sisters had helped shape his low opinion of women. They didn't stick around when there was something more exciting elsewhere. Lots of people were like that, and he supposed that was fine. But her attitude about Uncle Roy seemed to be the same deal as well. Unless there was something in it for her, she wasn't really interested.

"I bought the house a few years ago."

"He gave it to you?" Her voice had gone up an octave. She worked as a teacher, and he sure hoped she wasn't in her classroom.

"No. I bought it. Paid an appraiser to come and I paid the full amount the man said it was worth."

"I suppose I can look those records up at the courthouse."

The back of his neck heated. "They're public records. Feel free."

Her voice softened. "I hope the old fellow makes it. Let me know if anything changes."

"Sure." After she came that close to accusing him of lying, and was more concerned about her inheritance than Uncle Roy's health...yeah, he'd probably still call her. She hadn't changed a bit from what she was growing up. Her attitude angered him, but he wasn't going to change her at this late date.

They hung up, and McKoy stood, restless.

Jillian wasn't like his sisters. She had compassion and a heart to help. But so many of the women in his life had wanted more than what he could give. It was natural for him to be concerned. Right?

He checked the time, deciding it was okay to go grab a bite to eat. But his phone buzzed as he reached for the curtains. It was an area code and number he didn't recognize.

"Hello?" He turned, walking by the blank monitors and sitting on the edge of the chair.

"McKoy?" a cultured woman's voice. It sounded familiar.

"Yeah," he said curtly.

"McKoy, it's me, Isabella."

His ex-fiancée? He stilled for a moment. How long had it been since he'd talked to her? Five years? Seven? They'd broken up a decade ago, but they hadn't fought, mostly because he'd not said anything when she flew back across the ocean with a new man in tow.

"What do you want?"

"I...I'm sorry to bother you."

He'd been too short. He took a breath, reaching for compassion and kindness. "Sorry. That was blunt. I'm just surprised."

"Of course. We haven't spoken in a while, I know."

He waited. Surely she didn't expect him to make small talk.

She sighed. "I suppose you're not going to make this easy for me, are you?"

And he continued to wait, having no idea what "this" was.

"I am applying for a job. A very prestigious job. I need character references. I've never seen an application that required this many. I was hoping I could put you down. Having a government employee as a reference would look good." Her voice dropped at the end.

It seemed like a really odd request to him. He'd not seen her for years, and now she wanted him to vouch for her?

She never could stand his silences. It didn't surprise him when she spoke again. "McKoy, don't pout. What was between Reuben and I was so passionate and hot, there was just no way I could do anything but follow my feelings. You do understand, darling?"

He hated it when she called him darling. Even when they were engaged, it felt condescending. "You're still together?"

"Heavens, no. That's part of the reason I'm calling you. When we split, he accused me of cheating, when it was actually him that cheated on me. But our friends, for the most part, believed him. They took his side and I became the bad guy."

She droned on, but McKoy only listened with half an ear, thinking how ironic it was that Isabella had cheated on him, then had the same thing happen to her. It didn't make him happy. Not in any way, but he did appreciate the irony.

Her babbling hadn't stopped when Jillian's head poked around the curtain and smiled. "Hey."

His heart warmed at the sight of her.

"Gotta go, Isabella." He cut right into her speech. Something about the government and biosecurity measures at bottling plants. Weird stuff.

Jillian's brows drew down.

"So, I can put you down?"

"You can. And I can vouch for your work ethic. But I'm not going to lie for you."

She sighed, probably with relief. "I knew you wouldn't. Not to my good, but you won't lie to make me look bad, either."

She had him pegged.

"You know, McKoy. I probably shouldn't admit this to you, but I wish I hadn't pawned that ring." Her voice was soft and a little wistful.

McKoy looked at Jillian. She held a paper bag, which he was betting contained food, and two bottles of water. Jillian hadn't changed, and she still wore her workout clothes, but she wouldn't have looked more beautiful to him if she'd had on a fancy dress with all the bells and whistles. He smiled at her, and she grinned back at him.

"You know, Isabella," he paused, letting his eyes trail over Jillian again, "I'm not sorry. Not in the slightest."

~~~

Jillian wasn't sure who Isabella was. She realized she didn't even know the names of McKoy's sisters. And there he was talking about moving to Brazil with her. Maybe she should point that out to him. He seemed to think he was boring and lacked excitement in his life.

That wasn't something a boring person would do.

But something in his tone told her Isabella wasn't a relative.

He stood as he shut the phone off. "You brought food."

"Yep. Figured you wouldn't turn it down."

"Figured right." He dug in the bag. "Did you eat?"

"Nope. I hurried as fast as I could. I think Uncle Roy is going to be fine, but I didn't want you to be here alone in case the news was bad." She had her hand out, handing him a bottle of water, but he stepped forward and wrapped his arms around her instead. She would never get tired of him holding her.

"Thank you."

His reaction seemed a little extreme. "Did something happen?"

"I just appreciate you thinking about more than yourself. I wanted you to know that."

The curtain slid and they broke apart, although McKoy kept an arm around her, holding her to his side.

Orderlies rolled Uncle Roy in on his gurney. He was grinning. As soon as she saw that, Jillian's heart relaxed. He would be okay.

Chapter 16

"Doc needs to look over the film, but I'm ready to go." His gaze caught on the bag in McKoy's hand. "I'm starving. Hope that's for me."

"I doubt they're going to let you eat until they know more of what's going on." The orderlies rolled his monitors in and hooked him up to the screens set up behind the bed. They nodded at McKoy's statement.

"Just a bit longer, Mr. Rodning. Soon as the doctor reads that film."

"Can he have some water?" Jillian asked, and McKoy knew he probably had hearts in his eyes when he looked at her.

"I'll ask the doctor, but I'm sure that will be fine. Just sip slowly." The orderlies walked out.

In the end, they confirmed the original suspicion. Uncle Roy had gotten a little dizzy, probably because of low blood sugar, and fallen. The doctor sent him home with a clean bill of health.

As they walked together holding hands while following Uncle Roy up the walk, McKoy said, "I'm probably going to skip the rest of the conference."

"I can stay with him if you want me to." She lifted a shoulder. "I know I can't drive, so maybe you'd rather have someone else?"

"No one else is volunteering," he said, his heart full. Because Jillian didn't drive, it would be more of an inconvenience for her to stay, since she'd have to get up early and walk home to feed her animals. "Are you sure you don't mind?"

"It would ease my worry to know that someone is here in case something happened to him. In the hospital, I kept thinking we were lucky that he'd fallen this morning and not last night. He could have lain on the floor for hours."

McKoy shivered inside. "That thought crossed my mind too, but let's not borrow trouble."

Uncle Roy made it to the steps, and they split apart without words, each going to one side of him to help him up. He'd been chipper in the hospital, but the trip seemed to have worn him out. He hadn't said much on the way home.

McKoy got the door, and Jillian steadied him as he walked carefully over the stoop. She bustled around the kitchen, getting him a glass of water and the medication he took at lunch. Then she cleaned up the dishes in the sink and watered the small plant they kept on the sill.

McKoy took the dogs out to the back yard and let them run around some, since they'd missed their morning exercise. Maybe it was because of talking to his sister and Isabella, but he couldn't help thinking about how Jillian pitched in, not because she thought it was going to get her anything, but because she cared for Uncle Roy.

It was inaccurate and wrong to judge one woman by what others had done. But that's really what he'd been doing all this time. His mother hadn't been happy or satisfied with his dad, and it went on down to his sisters, then his fiancée.

Even now, as he'd gotten closer to Jillian, there was a part of him holding back, wondering if he wasn't making a mistake by trusting her. If today would be the day when she decided that he was boring and there wasn't enough in it for her and she was leaving.

He wasn't sure if he could shake that habit in one day, but he did know that she didn't deserve it.

~~~

Jillian sat with Uncle Roy in the living room until he fell asleep on the sofa. McKoy had seemed preoccupied and had been in and out, but hadn't said much.

But as Uncle Roy snored softly in the background, and Jillian started to think about going home, since she had classes in a couple of hours, he came to the doorway of the living room and said, "Come outside with me for a minute?"

His blue eyes were dark, and although his expression wasn't unkind, he wasn't smiling. She didn't know him well enough to be able to figure out what he wanted.

He held the door for her and she slipped through, walking over and sitting down on the swing.

Following her silently, he sat next to her, putting his arm around her back. She moved a little closer until their sides were touching and she was snuggled against him.

"Feels weird to be home in the middle of the afternoon on a weekday," he said at last, rocking the swing gently with his foot.

"I'm usually home, but I don't usually get to sit down and do nothing." She wasn't happy Uncle Roy had been in the ER, but she didn't mind the break. Sometimes she felt like she never stopped moving. She wanted her business to be successful, so she wouldn't change it, but she could appreciate the down time.

"I think I'll stay here the rest of the day and drive out early in the morning. If I left now, I'd barely get there before they're done."

"That's good. I have classes this afternoon. I know they said he was fine, but I feel better if someone is keeping an eye on him."

His fingers toyed in her hair. It seemed so casual, but intimate at the same time. "Yeah. Me too."

Then she remembered. with him leaving, she'd never told him what she'd overheard. "Monday, when I was at the post office, I overheard Todd talking to someone about an elephant and bribes. Something about a big game preserve. I couldn't really figure out what they were saying. Not enough to go to the police or even to know what to look for. It just felt off to me."

He'd stiffened beside her. "Who was he talking to?"

"I don't know. I was around the corner of the building, then Gail Patton came and I was embarrassed to be caught eavesdropping. By the time I was done talking to her, they were gone."

"I see."

"Oh, and before I forget, Gail's bringing her son over on Friday. I know we're going out, but it needs to be later."

His body softened beside her. "We can change it to tonight."

"Oh." Nerves flashed through her stomach. Although why she'd be nervous was beyond her. "I can do that."

"If you don't want to, it's fine."

She turned to see him watching her intently. "I want to. What makes you think I wouldn't?"

"You sounded a little strangled."

Her lips curved up. "The idea makes me nervous."

Those lines appeared between his eyes. "We're together now, so I assume it's not me that makes you nervous?"

"I've never been on a date."

His eyes widened. The lines deepened and she could almost see the wheels turning in his head. "Now I feel pressure. If this is your first date, I want it to be special."

She laughed. "There's no pressure. There's no competition." She looked out across the yard, thinking about the many times she'd listened to the older girls at the circus talk about their dates, either recent or, more likely, dates they'd had in their previous life somewhere else, more glamorous and exciting. It seemed that wherever one wasn't was more glamorous and exciting than wherever one was.

Without really thinking, she said, "I've always wanted to go to a drive-in."

"There's one not too far from here, but I think it's only open on the weekends." He was quiet for a moment. "Maybe I can figure something out."

She really couldn't say it, but she didn't care what they did on their date, as long as it included kissing at the end.

As the swing rocked slowly back and forth, she worried her lip, thinking that if he weren't planning on kissing her tonight, she would be disappointed. Would it be better to tell him what she expected so he knew?

"Um, McKoy?"

"Yeah?"

"I think the most important thing about a date is the goodnight kiss." There. She felt brave.

The swing stopped. The fingers gently stroking her hair froze.

"Really?" Now his voice sounded strangled.

"Yes."

"Hmm. Now I'm really feeling pressure. Maybe I should practice."

She grinned. "I think that's a great idea."

He chuckled. "I think I like the feeling of anticipation."

The swing started moving again.

Out of nowhere, he said, "My fiancée called and wanted a character reference."

"Isabella?"

"Yeah."

"I wondered if that's who you were talking to." She had been more worried that he wasn't telling her about it.

"I also told my sister that you...were my girlfriend." He paused. "I wasn't sure if that was accurate."

"I like the sound of that."

"Me too." He seemed about to say more, but the only sound was the creaking of the swing chains.

Eventually it was time for her classes, so after checking on Uncle Roy, who was still sleeping, McKoy took her home.

Chapter 17

A fter McKoy dropped her off, he got straight to work. The only drive-in in the area was open weekends, so if they were going to go to a "drive-in" he was going to have to make it himself.

It wasn't hard to find a white sheet, and he borrowed his church's projector. After fixing an early supper for Uncle Roy, he showered and changed. He hadn't been on many dates since his fiancée had dumped him. He had to admit, he was nervous, too.

Her last class was over at six. He showed up early and enjoyed watching her work with the people and their dogs. She stood with her back to him, using a hyper golden retriever to show the students how to do "stay." He laughed as the dog practically trembled beside her, but it stayed in place.

Again he was amazed at how good she was with animals. She never raised her voice, and they seemed to want to do everything they could to please her.

"You'll want to take it slow. Don't tell them to stay, then think you can leave the room. For this week, if you can get them to stay while you walk slowly around them, I would consider that a win." As she spoke, she held the retriever's leash in one hand and took a step out, walking slowly around the animal. It quivered, but held its butt on the floor position. Its head swiveled as she turned slowly.

She stepped back in place and paused for a second, before saying, "Okay." The dog bounded up, jumping and dancing. Jillian laughed, and petted it, murmuring what a good dog it was before taking the lead and walking it back to its owner.

"That's it for today. I'll see you all next week. Practice the 'stay' command."

People slowly started to leave, taking time to chat a bit with Jillian. McKoy knew she normally checked the kenneled dogs' water and did a last cleaning, so he ducked out and started that work for her. He was in the last dog's pen with a shovel when she came out.

"Hey, you didn't have to do that." She bent and petted the poodle mix. It leaned against her, its eyes closed in bliss.

"I know. I wanted to." He grinned at her, and she returned his smile. "The sooner your work is done, the sooner I get you to myself."

"What about Uncle Roy?" She craned her head to look up at him while continuing to scratch the dog.

"He's had supper and he's doing good. He was pretty happy when I told him I was spending the evening with you. I think he'd be thrilled if I moved out and you moved in." He dumped his shovel load in the bin and leaned it against the wall before checking the automatic waterer.

Jillian gave the poodle mix a last pat. "I like Uncle Roy."

"I highly doubt that you like him as much as he likes you." McKoy lifted his brows and Jillian laughed as they walked out and shut the door.

"I'll need to get a shower," she said as they shut the lights out and locked up.

"That's fine. It's a nice evening. I'll sit on your porch." The peepers were singing and a few birds tweeted in the fading light.

"I won't be long. What should I wear?"

"No need to get fancy." Indicating his jeans and button-up, he said, "I'm wearing this." He took her hand as they walked through the yard, wishing he could tell the future. Would she go to Brazil? What would become of Heidi? He wanted to know that they would have a future together. But he couldn't. All he could do was to try to have the best time he could tonight. Tomorrow was another day.

True to her word, she showered and was back out the door in less than twenty minutes. Her long hair was still damp, and she wore flip flops with jeans and a loose, peasant blouse.

He'd been sitting on the stoop, petting Snickers, who was curled beside him with her nose on his leg. The sky had exploded in decadent colors of orange and pink and blue, and the gradual changing of light and colors always fascinated him.

When the door creaked, he turned, getting ready to make some comment about the beauty of the sky. Maybe it was her damp hair. Or the freshness of her face. Or maybe the graceful way she moved in her jeans.

Whatever it was, his tongue stuck to the roof of his mouth, and whatever he'd been going to say flew completely out of his brain.

He tried to swallow, but his mouth was dry. He couldn't get any words out.

He cleared his throat and tried again. "You're beautiful."

She gave a tentative smile. "I know you're just being kind. You said not to get fancy."

If she rendered him speechless in her casual clothes... He shoved his hands in his pockets. "I don't think I could handle you 'fancy.'"

Snickers went over and nosed at her leg. "Sorry, you're staying here." She gave the dog a pat on the head, then looked up at McKoy. "You ready?"

"Yeah. I'm feeling like I have the most beautiful woman in the world with me tonight, and I don't deserve it." He held his hand out and she took it. She wasn't just beautiful on the inside.

"You're not exactly a slouch. Didn't you see how that lady with the dalmatian was looking at you?"

"Huh? I remember seeing the dalmatian, but are you sure the handler was a woman?"

Jillian snorted as they stepped off the stoop. "She sure was, and that was how I knew you were there. Of course, the dogs all looked at you, so I knew someone was behind me, but the dalmatian lady's eyes widened, then she started drooling, so I figured—"

"Drooling? Okay, sounds like a fairy tale to me."

"Okay, so I exaggerated a little on the drooling. But, seriously, I could tell she was looking at you. Women do that, you know."

"No." He really didn't know. He opened his truck door and helped her up, closing it behind her and walking around.

He pulled out of her drive, waving at Fink and Ellie as they sat on their porch swing, Ellie cradled under Fink's arm as they watched the sun setting. Their boys rode bikes in the drive and McKoy carefully maneuvered past them, waving at each of the boys in turn.

"Where are we going?" Jillian asked as they pulled out on the highway.

Nerves bunched in his stomach again. He hoped she wasn't disappointed that they weren't going anywhere. He wasn't experienced in the dating game and what had seemed like a really great idea a few hours ago seemed lame and cheap now.

"You said you wanted to go to a drive-in. But there aren't any that are open tonight. So I made my own."

"You made your own drive-in?"

"Yeah." He swallowed. "We'll have to pop our own popcorn, and I have hotdogs. Figured we'd get ice cream after the movie. But we can do something else if you want. I was just kind of thinking that maybe it wasn't the great idea I thought it was earlier."

"It sounds fabulous. How are we going to watch the movie?"

"You'll see."

It wasn't far to his house and he pulled into his drive a moment later. But instead of parking in front of his house like he normally did, he pulled around back and drove along the fenced yard. A small creek bordered the back of their property, with trees lining it. He'd found two trees the perfect width apart and hung the sheet between them.

His headlights hit it and it glowed white.

"Oh, my! You hung your own screen?" Jillian hopped up and down on the seat.

"I was going to park the truck here and we'll walk back and make our food." He pulled around, turning and backing toward the screen. He'd already stretched out the extension cord he'd need for the projector. He'd tried it all earlier and had gotten it to work perfectly.

He'd never get tired of holding her hand, and he grabbed it as they walked back through the yard. "So, is growing up in the circus a good way to spend a childhood?" he asked, wanting to know everything about her.

Maybe they wouldn't be together forever. But that made him all the more determined to not waste a second learning about her.

"I suppose." Her fingers tightened in his. "Actually, yes. I loved growing up in the circus. I love the things I learned. It makes me different than anyone I know, but a good different."

"But?" He could tell by her tone there was a "but."

"What I really missed was having a dad. You know? I used to dream he'd show up and we'd be a family. I'd dream he'd want me. That he'd come see me perform and recognize me as his daughter right away. So many dreams about my dad."

"You don't have any idea who he is?"

"Nope. Not even a name, other than Powell. I'm not sure my mom knew his name, to be honest." She swung their hands. He figured to try to show that she didn't care, when it was obvious she did.

"I vowed I would never have a child that didn't have a father."

They stepped up on the porch, but he didn't open the door. He waited for her to keep talking.

"I wanted a dad so much." She ran a hand along her hair, pushing it behind her shoulder. "There were older guys in the circus who kind of stepped in and helped fill that role, but it wasn't the same, you know?"

"Yeah." He thought of his mother who left. His sisters hadn't even really tried to be the mother he longed for.

He'd wanted a mother more than anything, just like Jillian had wanted a dad. He hadn't gone as far as determining that he'd never raise a child without a mother, but he supposed when he pretty much cut himself off from dating after his fiancée dumped him, that was probably what his subconscious was saying.

"I wondered why he didn't stay, you know?" she said softly. "Did he miss America? Was he only passing through? Maybe he died?"

"Wouldn't your mother tell you?" McKoy thought that was a little mean. Surely now Jillian's mother could face whatever mistake she made and tell Jillian what she could of her father.

"I stopped asking, even before I was a teenager. No point. Because her answers were always the same."

"You should try again."

"Yeah. Maybe I'll do that."

He hoped she could get the answers she needed. "Now that you're older, maybe she can be convinced that you need to know."

Jillian nodded. "I haven't thought about it in a while. A long while. I've been more focused, first on what I was going to do when the circus dissolved, then on getting into America and figuring out how to pay everyone I owe..."

He'd forgotten about her debts. "I just bought Uncle Roy's house last year. I used all the money I had in savings to pay cash for it, then last summer I had a new roof put on and the furnace replaced."

The light coming out the door shone on her quizzical expression.

"I'm telling you that to say that I don't have the money in hand to pay the debts you owe, but I can easily get a loan, even if I have to use the house as collateral, to pay the men you owe."

"You can't do that."

"Why not?"

"I won't let you."

He opened the door, but she didn't walk through. He put his hand on her back. She walked under his pressure, but her face frowned.

"I want to do it," he said.

"No."

"Jillian, I can help you. Let me."

Uncle Roy was not in the kitchen. He'd probably taken his dogs and retired to his room already.

"Let's not fight about it tonight."

He didn't intend to fight about it at all. He intended to give her the money to take care of it. Even if she went to Brazil. It would ease his mind to know that there were no drug dealers after her for their exorbitant fees for getting her across the border and into PA.

He nodded. "There's the popcorn." He indicated the popper. "I'll heat some hot dogs up."

He hated that they'd been arguing over the money. He hadn't wanted the evening to be a fight.

"Did you ever have trouble with the elephants? Either in your act or handling them in general?"

The popcorn whirled in the background as her black eyes flashed at him. "Nope. Not a single one. But Florin, the man who trained them, said that they'd do anything if you gained their respect. He didn't use a lot of the heavy-handed tactics that other trainers did. We joked that he was the elephant whisperer."

"So that's where you got it."

"Got what?"

"I was just watching you tonight, thinking about how good you were with animals. Any animals. That retriever tonight... I was shocked that it stayed. Its body didn't want to."

She laughed, and her scent of cotton candy drifted over the popping corn and cooking hotdogs. "Its body didn't, but its mind wanted to please me."

"Exactly. How do you cast your spell?"

"Oh, don't you know a magician can't tell his secrets?"

She looked so perfect in his kitchen, smiling and laughing. Natural. Like there wasn't a place in the world where she belonged more.

Or maybe he just didn't want her to belong anywhere else.

He shook his head and grabbed the hot dog buns.

They laughed as they put lots of butter and salt on the popcorn and he loaded the hotdogs up with onions and relish. Sticking two bottles of water under his arm, they carried their bounty to his truck.

"Maybe you've seen this movie?" he asked as the popular one about elephants and a circus started to play.

"I have, but I'd love to watch it again with you," she said. And he believed her. She looked at him like he was something special. And it made him want to be special, just to live up to the look in her eye.

He'd spread blankets out on the back of his truck and when they were done eating, they leaned against the back of the cab. She tucked in close to him, and he put his arm around her, pulling her even closer, resting his cheek on her soft hair.

He froze when her hand dropped to his leg, but it just lay there, although he could feel the burn the whole way through his jeans. A sweet burn.

He knew there was an elephant in their movie and a train, but he wasn't sure what the rest of it was about. He'd chosen it for Jillian anyway.

It had gotten chilly since the sun went down, and by the time the movie ended they had a blanket spread over their legs. He turned the projector and computer off, and they sat in the back of his truck, their faces turned up to the clear sky where stars of various brightness twinkled down at them.

How long had it been since he'd just stared up at the night sky? He loved watching the sunrise and the sunset, but he'd forgotten how pretty the starry sky could be. Or maybe it was Jillian beside him that heightened his senses and made him appreciate everything more than normal.

The fresh, country air. The swish of the wind through the trees and the peepers calling from the stream. The lingering scent of popcorn and butter. And a covering of celestial beauty.

"It's a perfect night," he said softly. "And I have the perfect company."

Her head rested on his shoulder. He didn't want to move.

"You've made it the perfect night. I couldn't imagine a better date." Her voice was low, content, with that little trace of accent that made it lyrical and unique.

He figured a lot of girls would have accused him of being cheap. That wasn't the intention. He'd tried to make it what she wanted.

"We'll have to go to the real drive-in sometime." That was assuming that they were even together. But he hated to ruin their time together talking about how soon it was going to end.

"Maybe you've spoiled me tonight, because I think the private drive-in that you created is better than anything else there could possibly be out there. Why would I want to go park amidst a bunch of people when I can be here, alone, with you?"

"That sounds kind of boring." Part of his heart shivered as he said that. It was one of his deepest insecurities. That he wasn't enough to keep a woman interested. Jillian hadn't seemed to be bothered, but maybe it would come in time.

Her body turned toward him, and her head lifted. Her hand touched the stubble on his face and slid along his cheek, cupping it.

His stomach tightened. He closed his eyes and took a breath before opening them and looking down at her.

Her dark eyes, reflecting the secrets of the universe, stared up at him. "Never boring. Just being next to you stirs so much tension and exhilaration in my soul, I can hardly stand it."

Her words made him shiver, but he couldn't move out of her hand.

When her eyes dropped to his lips, sparks shot through his body, and he lifted his own hand, cupping her cheek before sliding his fingers through her soft hair, feeling it slip across his callouses.

She'd already said she wanted him to kiss her, so he didn't even think about asking permission. But doing it in such a way that he didn't lose control was his main focus. The privacy of having their own little world here in his backyard worked against him in that regard.

He lowered his head. The corners of her lips turned up and her eyes drifted closed. Her body pressed into his and her hand on his cheek slid around until it was tugging at his neck, urging him closer.

His lips hovered just above hers. "One kiss with you feels like a hundred more," he said, his voice coming out rougher than he intended.

"I'm okay with a hundred." Her breath whispered against his lips and his whole body wanted to pull her even closer.

He breathed out a puff of air. It didn't sound like she was going to help him keep the fire between them banked. "I need your help. Just a kiss." There couldn't be more. Not tonight. Not when he knew she could be leaving anytime. Not when he didn't have a prayer of making her his.

"Make it a long one," she said before she closed the sliver of space between them, her lips soft and hungry against his even hungrier ones.

He recognized the riot of emotions that flew through his body and the almost uncontrollable urge to pull her closer, to touch her and fit her body against his. Stronger than the last time and just as wild. His hand buried in her hair and he focused on her lips and the sweet taste of her mouth, pushing back against that drive in him to have more, take more, turn the kiss into more.

What felt like a long time later, he dropped his forehead against hers and took big breaths of sweet night air, trying to corral his runaway emotions, heightened, no doubt, by the idea that wasn't far from his mind—she could be leaving. He might never see her again.

Her hands played with the short hair at the base of his neck, and somehow he'd dragged her body across his so she sat in his lap.

When he thought his throat had opened enough for him to speak without squeaking, he said, "That's not something I want to attempt standing up."

She gave a light laugh. Her lips touched his forehead, then trailed down his face, along his jaw, before touching his lightly, quickly. She leaned back. "Me either." Her chest moved deeply, in and out. "You're right. One feels like a hundred more."

Her hands framed his cheeks. "Thank you."

He lifted a brow, his hands sliding down her graceful back to her waist. "For the kiss? That should be me thanking you. I don't have enough experience to know how to kiss and make the entire world disappear."

She snorted. "For the kiss and the date. And I did sneak a few kisses out behind the big top, but the excitement of hoping I didn't get caught was greater than whatever thrill I got from the kiss. I don't think you can blame me for the disappearance of the world."

His hands had tightened at the thought of someone else kissing her. It was hard to think like that, but he had to let her go. Had to face the fact that it wouldn't be him holding her and kissing her in Brazil.

He shook those thoughts out of his head. He wanted to live in the moment. Enjoy what he had before it was gone. They snuggled there for a little longer, but it was late, and they both had early starts to their day.

They folded the blankets, kissing cheeks and shoulders and foreheads, laughing as they bumped into each other, and purposely avoiding touching lips. Until it ended all too soon, and they were at her porch, Snickers whining at their feet. McCoy had to shove his hands in his pockets so he didn't hold her and not let her go.

"I'm driving back out to Somerset in the morning. I missed today, but I can catch tomorrow and Friday morning."

"I figured. I'll keep an eye on Uncle Roy."

"If you want to sleep there, you're welcome to. But I know you have to be here, too."

"Yeah. It's not a big deal to run over." She crossed her arms over her chest.

"I appreciate it."

"I'm glad you do, but I like Uncle Roy and I'm glad I can help."

"You're cold. Go inside."

"Call me again, please? I...I liked hearing from you."

Her words made him smile. "You can call me, you know."

"Yeah. I don't want to bother you if you're in a session or if, you know, if you do something after."

He hated the insecurity in her words. There was no need for it. He took the step and closed the distance between them, putting his arms around her and pulling her into him. "I don't care who I'm with or what I'm doing. You're the one I'm thinking about. All day." He clenched his jaw. "All night."

Kissing her again was not his smartest move, but her arms went around him and her face lifted and he bent his head, his hands holding her close as everything else faded away. She pressed against him and held on like she never wanted to let go.

He didn't want to let go, either. But he pulled away, then backed up, his hands dropping, his heart racing. "Go on," he said, wanting to see her safely in before he drove away.

She didn't say anything more but turned and fled into her house.

His heart hurt as he turned away, but what else was there to do? He couldn't press her for a decision or a commitment. He was already way out of his comfort zone, operating without even knowing if she would still be living in the country this time next week.

Heck, he was way out of his comfort zone the second she admitted she wasn't legal.

When his phone buzzed before he'd made it to the blacktop road, he grinned, thinking it was Jillian, unable to wait to call.

But it was Gator. "Hello?"

"McKoy. Sorry about the late phone call. Hope I'm not waking you up."

"Nah." He wasn't going to get into where he was and what he was doing.

"My wife has ganged up against me with my mother, and they've decided they want a garden." It was easy to hear the good-natured humor in his friend's voice. "Do you mind if I borrow your tiller?"

"Sure it's in the shed. I'll tell Uncle Roy you might be around. I'll be out for the rest of the week." Something triggered in the back of his mind. Gator had been working in Montana and his wife, Avery, had commitments out east, if he remembered correctly.

"I'll probably be over tomorrow after work."

"That's fine." He was speaking again before he'd given it a lot of thought. "You were in Montana and Avery was out east. How'd you guys work that out?"

Sure he'd been in Gator's wedding, but they were far more likely to talk about what type of tree stand worked better in the rain, or what type of shot he was packing in his twenty-gage shells than anything even remotely resembling a relationship question.

McKoy felt foolish for even asking.

But Gator didn't laugh or hesitate. "You know. I thought that was going to be a problem. There aren't a whole lot of orchestras in Montana. And I had no interest in going out east. But it's funny, when you really want to figure something out, suddenly options open up that you might never have thought of in an ordinary situation." Gator laughed. "There wasn't any way I was going to let her get away. I was ready to do whatever it took. She felt the same way. I think when we realized the sacrifice we were each willing to make for the other, it didn't feel like a sacrifice anymore. It felt like giving up something we wanted for something even better."

McKoy had reached his driveway by this time and had parked in front of his house, sitting in his truck with his elbows on his steering wheel, trying to process what Gator was saying.

When you wanted something bad enough you made it work?

Or, sacrifices don't feel like sacrifices when what you're giving up feels like less than what you're getting?

He wasn't sure he understood.

"Okay." He wasn't sure what else to say.

"Yeah, it's crazy." Gator barely paused before he said, "I want to shoot my crossbow before spring gobbler. Maybe we can meet at the gun range sometime next week."

They were back on familiar ground and spent a few minutes discussing the regulations on crossbows in turkey season before they hung up.

But McKoy's mind hadn't really wandered from what Gator had said about considering things he hadn't thought were possibilities before. He'd already done that by being with Jillian in the first place. What else could he do?

Chapter 18

Louie called early the next morning as McKoy was making coffee in the predawn darkness.

He answered on the first ring. "Hello?"

"Hey, figured you'd be up. Is everything okay with your uncle?"

"Yes. We brought him home yesterday, and he's sleeping now."

"Anything serious?"

"Doctor said it was low blood sugar that made him dizzy. So, sounds like not." McKoy was pretty sure his boss wasn't calling at this time in the morning to make pleasant conversation, so he braced himself.

"Well, I was planning on taking you and Todd out last night and telling you, but my position, the supervisor promotion, is going to him."

The news didn't shock McKoy, he'd been expecting this, but it did make his chest contract and his stomach sink. Especially after the scare with Uncle Roy, it would be nice to not have to travel.

"Good for him." McKoy couldn't think of anything else to say.

"You're going to be working under him. Is that going to be a problem?"

McKoy pulled his mug out of the cupboard. "No."

He didn't know how things were going with Jillian. Which reminded him of the conversation she'd overheard. He'd forgotten all about it in the comfort of holding her close on the swing and thinking about spending the evening with her and their date. Kissing her.

"I can have you transferred. I understand that sometimes when you've been coworkers, it's hard to switch it to boss and employee."

It would be worse to be transferred. "There won't be any problems."

They hung up shortly after.

Once he started thinking about that conversation, he couldn't get the idea of a bribe out of his head.

Surely Louie wasn't involved.

But he didn't have a problem believing that Todd was, somehow. Jillian wasn't imagining the conversation she overheard, and "bribe" was a pretty strong word. But without evidence...

Everyone from the office would be at the conference.

Loretta would be in today, but not until nine. The place would be deserted.

Todd probably wouldn't have left evidence lying around. But McKoy couldn't stop the restless irritation that burned in his body. Plus, he'd be driving right by the office on his way back to the conference. What could it hurt to stop and look around?

A bribe. A big game preserve. What else had Jillian heard? And how did it fit?

Heidi had one tusk. Surely they wouldn't kill her for that? Did people kill elephants for sport? He wasn't sure, but he knew there was a black market for animals that he would have never considered being valuable or traded. In his line of work, he'd seen a lot of things that he wouldn't have believed if he hadn't been there himself.

He poured his coffee and settled the lid on his cup. He'd peeked in Uncle Roy's room on his way down, and the old man had been snoring loudly.

McKoy grabbed his cup and walked out of the house.

His mind hadn't changed in the thirty-minute drive, and he pulled into the deserted office parking lot just as the sun started its slow climb out from behind the eastern mountains.

He met the cleaning lady on the way out. "Oh," she said in surprise as she struggled through the door with a large bag of trash. "I thought I would get this done this morning rather than last night since everyone was out for the day."

She pushed the door with her hip.

"My kids had a recital last night." She shook her head. "I'm almost finished. Just need to throw this away."

Only Louie had a key to the building, so he was glad he'd met her. He grabbed the open door. "If you set that trash bag down, I'll see that it gets to the dumpster." Hopefully, his offer would distract her from the fact that he was getting in because of her having the door open.

"Oh, well thanks. It's killing my shoulder to throw these big bags in."

She let the garbage sit on the stoop and ducked back in the building. McKoy made a mental note to remember to throw it away and strode in, going first to his office.

Just as he'd left it. Pretty bare. He'd never be a paperwork person.

He heard the side door close behind the cleaning lady and walked to a hall window, peering out as her car left the lot. Empty.

Feeling like a criminal, he pushed on Louie's door. It slid open silently. This would be Todd's office soon. He didn't feel any jealousy, necessarily. Sometimes things went his way and sometimes they didn't. But he did feel like maybe Todd didn't deserve the promotion. He came late, left early, and got out of as much work as he could. But he was good at schmoozing with the boss. McKoy never had a chance if that was a requirement for promotion.

There were papers and books scattered all over Louie's desk. McKoy didn't even really know what he was looking for. It was a dumb idea to come in in the first place.

He couldn't root through his boss's drawers. Or anywhere else for that matter. With a last glance at the desk that held nothing of interest, he walked out of the office and closed the door behind him.

Standing in the reception area, he considered Todd's office door. Should he? He'd felt like a trespasser in Louie's office, Todd's probably wouldn't be much different. But what was the point in stopping in if he didn't check?

Unfortunately, he couldn't do it. He hated the idea of Todd going into his office and snooping through his stuff, and he couldn't do it to Todd. Maybe he was missing incriminating evidence, but that's the way it would be.

He had a policeman buddy that he'd worked with on various cases, including the dog fighting ring he'd been chasing leads on for a while. He had a few things he needed to discuss with him. Maybe he could ask if there was anything that could be done, maybe a little side investigation to see if anything panned out.

Feeling like he'd failed Jillian, he walked out of the office building, making sure the door was locked behind him.

The bag of garbage he'd promised the cleaning lady he'd throw away sat on the stoop. He picked it up, then paused. Maybe he could look in it?

The parking lot was empty, facing an empty field and a row of trees. A strong urge compelled him to untie the string and pry open the bag.

A printed money wire sat on the top.

McKoy picked it out carefully and looked at it. Fifty grand. Todd's name and a name he didn't recognize. "Elephant purchase" was written in the notes section and it had a date from last week on it.

Rather than call his cop buddy, McKoy decided he'd stop at the station on his way back to the conference.

Chapter 19

Jillian woke up with a smile on her face. Last night had been the most amazing night of her life. McKoy didn't seem like the romantic type—he wasn't the romantic type—but he'd made a huge effort to do something nice for her, and he'd seemed to enjoy it just as much as she had. And kissing him...wow.

She put a finger to her lips, like they might be different this morning than they'd been before. They felt different. Better.

It was Thursday and she had to go a whole day until she'd see him tomorrow afternoon. If she saw him then. She wanted to call him, or text. Wanted to spend every waking second with him.

But she had a business to run and an elephant to tend to, then she needed to check on Uncle Roy.

Her happy bubble dipped slightly, and she threw her legs out of bed. Her heart was still full from last night and she wouldn't soon forget the image of McKoy's deep blue eyes, hot and heavy lidded as his face lowered toward hers...

Her phone buzzed. She leaped toward it, thinking maybe it was McKoy calling, but it was an international call. She steeled herself and swiped.

"*Bueno.*"

"Jillian. This is Ricardo. I'm not sure if you remember me..."

She remembered him. He'd worked in the circus. He'd been in several acts—everyone was—but he'd also been in charge of procuring feed for the animals and buying and replacing exotics. He was some relation to the owners. She'd tried to stay away from him as much as possible, because her mother had said that he was probably involved with the cartels that ran everything down there. They assumed he could not be so deeply involved with the administrative side of the circus and not be involved with the cartels.

Basically, her mother hadn't trusted him, so neither had she. But he was nice, and she liked him.

"I do," she said. He didn't need to know everything she remembered or thought.

"I've been hearing that you did not get my letter that should have arrived with Heidi."

"No." So he was the one who had sent her the elephant.

"My carriers just arrived back yesterday. They told me there were a lot of people at your place when they dropped her off. They were afraid of the police. We cannot bribe them."

She smiled, thinking of McKoy. His honesty and integrity. Very appealing.

"They laid low for a bit, but they said you seemed to have everything under control."

She didn't bother to stop her eyeroll. "It's an elephant! I can't afford to keep an elephant."

"Didn't they give you the money?"

"What money?"

"It was hard enough to send one elephant—we put her in an auto car on the train and faked the papers. Thankfully there aren't any inspections, and there is a rail siding on a local line not two miles from your farm. The people who own that usually unload feed and fertilizer, but they let us borrow it for a night. My men were able to walk the elephant to your place from there." He stopped to take a breath. "I had to sell Hazel to pay for Heidi. But I sent the rest of the money along, because I know it's expensive to feed them."

"I didn't see any money. But it doesn't matter. Hazel isn't doing well."

"Oh?" He sounded surprised.

"The man in Brazil who bought her said she's not eating."

"I see." He sounded as concerned as she felt.

"They're sisters and they've never been separated."

"I know. I didn't realize it would be that bad." There was some talking in the background. "I have to go. I will look into this further and call you back. By this weekend at the latest."

Jillian could remember Ricardo's compassion. He wasn't one of the men who didn't care about the animals, nor one who was always walking around with a stick, making sure everyone knew and respected his authority. She had confidence that he would truly look into the issue and honestly try to fix things.

She thanked him and they hung up.

Thursday went by slowly. McKoy called her on the lunch break, and they talked until after his afternoon session started. They spoke again for several hours that night. She wouldn't have thought she could spend hours on the phone, but they didn't lack for things to talk about.

Friday he called when the morning session was over just to tell her that he couldn't come straight home because he had a business lunch he had to get through first.

She supposed it shouldn't have surprised her when, two hours later, Todd's car came flying down the drive and pulled up to the barn where she'd just cleaned Heidi's large enclosure and was putting the elephant back in.

She locked the gate and turned to face him.

He got out of his car with a smirk. "Afternoon. Nice day."

"Sure is," she said.

"I'm here to do an unscheduled inspection. You don't need to stay if you have work to do." He pulled out a clipboard and slammed his car door shut.

She had a class that was starting in less than an hour, but she shrugged. "I can hang around."

Irritation flashed across his features, but he gave her a tight-lipped smile. "No more dog bites?"

"No."

"That's good. The powers that be don't like to see complaints coming from your property when you're trying to get a permit. Only," he tilted his head like the thought had just occurred to him. "You're not trying to get a permit. Are you?"

She held his gaze. "I have thirty days."

"I asked if you were trying to get a permit."

She didn't want to make an enemy of this man, but she didn't want to give him a reason to take Heidi. The exact way he'd said "big game preserve" came back to her clearly. She straightened. Not only was Heidi in danger, if Todd had any clue that she was less legal than her elephant, he'd have DHS on the farm before her next class started. She'd bet on it.

"Yes. I'm trying." It wasn't a complete lie. She had tried. She'd just stopped before she even got started when she realized she needed to be a citizen.

"Hmm. Funny that I can't find your name in the system," he said, to himself as much as to her, which made her wonder if he'd tried to break into the system somehow and sabotage her permit application, since there wasn't anything that he could legitimately fail her for in his inspection.

"Is Jillian your real name?"

"Yes."

"And you've applied for a permit?"

A car pulled down the drive, and he turned from her to check it out. Almost like he was afraid... It hit her that he thought McKoy might be coming.

She felt that thought was right on the money, because he turned and said, "I'm going to get started with the inspection. You're not allowed to follow me around."

Pretty sure he made that last part up, she was also sure that he wanted to get it over with before McKoy was there to watch him. He must not know McKoy had a meeting.

"Too bad your boyfriend didn't get the promotion," he said as he started toward the gate.

She stood where she was, beside the car, leaning on the shovel. When had McKoy found out about that? Maybe he didn't know. He hadn't said anything to her and they'd talked for hours last night.

Todd had his back to her, and she didn't bother talking to it. She'd see McKoy soon enough. Todd walked around the enclosure and out of sight. Wanting to follow, but not wanting to upset him, she couldn't figure out what he was doing that was taking so long.

Finally, cars started arriving for her class and she walked to the kennel building. Gail Patton would be there with Bennett shortly after class.

Dread and anxiety swirled in Jillian's stomach. Surely Todd wouldn't fail her and take Heidi today. She'd have a day at least to call Mario in Brazil. Trouble was, as soon as she did, she knew she'd have to agree to go down, and she didn't want to leave McKoy.

She made it through her class, trying hard to concentrate, but having trouble.

Sometime during her class, Todd left. He didn't stop. She never even saw him.

She didn't know what that meant, but hoped that she'd at least have until Monday before the government moved. McKoy hadn't come. He hadn't said whether he'd stop here on his way home or check on Uncle Roy first.

The last student had barely left the drive when Gail's small car pulled in. Her son practically bounded out of the backseat and he'd run around the car twice before Gail got out and stood.

Jillian had to laugh. What a cute little boy. The school district was probably after Gail to medicate that one.

He gave his hand easily to his mother, but jumped beside her as she strode to the kennels.

Jillian put the last of the paperwork away, still smiling at the little boy. Unbidden, a thought came to her. What would McKoy's son look like? Blue eyes? Blond hair? That strong jaw. His height? The broad shoulders.

She could see a miniature McKoy in her mind's eye, easily. A longing to be the mother of that little one, and maybe a sister to go along with him, pulled hard at her insides.

She tried to shake it, but one glance at the little guy who was still jumping, now on one foot at a time, brought it back.

Walking out of the kennel, she held her hand out to Gail. "I'm so glad you could come."

"Thanks so much for having us. Bennett is excited. To say the least." She gave her hopping and skipping son a loving mother's glance.

"Looks like it. I'm done here and we can walk over."

They started over, Bennett skipping along, and Gail and Jillian talking about the nice weather.

A white paper stuck to the metal rails caught Jillian's eye, and her voice trailed off in the middle of making a comment about the height of the corn and the last frost date.

She hurried to the gate, staring at the paper, but not touching it. There were only two words on it, big and black: Failed Inspection.

Although she'd suspected that's what he was going to do, it hit her in the chest and made her whole body feel heavy and wrong.

"What's that?" Gail asked, coming up beside her.

"I had an inspection with animal control today." She didn't bother explaining about the permit. "I've passed every one so far, but it looks like today I didn't."

"That's odd. What's the problem?"

"I don't know. The area has to be clean. There has to be feed and water. The fence has to be in place. Everything that I know about is in good order." She didn't want to pull Gail into her problems, so she shrugged. "Let's see if we can get Heidi to come over so Bennett can pet her. I'll do a few things with her, then we'll see if Bennett wants to ride. Will that work?"

"Yes! Yes! Yes!" Bennett jumped up and down and fist pumped the air.

She slipped in the gate, not ripping the offending paper off by the barest of control, and walked slowly over to Heidi, petting her and giving her a carrot from her pocket.

Giving the command, she stepped onto Heidi's trunk, and rode it out to the gate. Bennett's eyes were as round as saucers, and Jillian had to laugh. One of the best parts of being a circus performer had been making people smile. Seeing Bennett's excitement and happiness breathed new life into her and helped her shove aside the issue of the failed inspection and the impending consequences.

Heidi seemed to enjoy the attention as well. She performed beautifully, allowing Jillian to put her harness on and do her routine in its entirety. Jillian lost herself in the flow of the moves and the heat of the elephant, the feeling that she'd become one with the animal and they were working in tandem. It was a beautiful thing when everything went right and the one move flowed into the next. Heidi knew her part and played it to perfection, like there were ten thousand people watching rather than one wide-eyed little boy and his tired, but happy, mother.

And a broad-shouldered man.

Jillian realized with a start as Heidi and she wrapped up their act that McKoy leaned against the fence as well. She gave him a tentative smile, a little nervous after not seeing him for two days.

His eyes were hot on her. They always were, but he'd had to have seen the sign, too.

She did a backbend, flipping over into a sitting position, before calling out, "Does Bennett want a ride?"

He was saying "yes" before the question was out of her mouth. McKoy unlocked the gate. "You want him in there?"

"Yes, please," she said, her voice softening on its own, which made him smile. Memories of their date and kiss flashed in her mind.

He took Bennett's hand and led him through the opening.

"Put your hand in front of her like this." Jillian put up the universal sign for stop.

McKoy obeyed.

"Hold him up."

McKoy picked Bennett up under his arms.

"Reach up," Jillian commanded.

Bennett put his arms in the air and Jillian grabbed his hands, pulling him up and settling him on in front of her.

"Now, just walk beside her with your palm away from her. When you want her to stop, point your palm toward her." Jillian settled Bennett better in front of her. For the first time since he set foot on the farm, he was actually still. "Make sure she can see it," she added.

McKoy gave her a raised brow.

She shrugged. Of course it was common sense. He grinned at her, and warm feelings stirred in her soul at the private words that flowed between them without them saying a thing.

McKoy did a perfect job of "leading" Heidi around, and Bennett seemed to enjoy his ride thoroughly. Gail was grateful and appreciative as she gathered her hopping and skipping son and walked to her car.

Jillian slid over Heidi's head and commanded her to let her down. McKoy was there and she stepped into his arms. She hadn't seen him for days and was ready to bury her head in his chest and cry out her frustration with Todd and everything else that was going on with Heidi.

She hadn't even thought about it, but Carlos would be calling again soon, asking about the money she owed him, which she'd spent on buying hay for Heidi.

McKoy seemed to realize she was holding him tighter than usual.

"What's the matter?"

"I'm just happy you're home."

"I forgot to say anything last night, but I didn't get the promotion."

"Todd told me when he came today." She leaned back a little. "I'm sorry."

"Maybe something else will work out," he said. He didn't seem angry, but she could see frustration on his face. She could understand that. Todd had failed her for no reason that she could see and had gotten a promotion. Didn't seem fair. But it also wasn't something she wanted to dwell on. So she nodded, but didn't comment.

"I didn't stop and see Uncle Roy. Are you almost done here? Want to go home with me and I'll figure out something for supper?"

Thrilled that he wanted to spend time with her, she remembered Bennett and stopped herself from hopping just like him in time. Instead, she grinned. "I'm finished and I'd love to."

He put his arm around her and they walked to the truck. If she could keep her mind from the decisions that inevitably had to be made this weekend, she could maybe just relax and enjoy the company of the man she couldn't stop thinking about.

After a supper of eggs with mushrooms and spinach and sausage, they played several rounds of cards. Jillian knew a few tricks from her years in the circus, but she didn't cheat, and McKoy beat them both every round. Uncle Roy took his dogs to his room.

McKoy stood at the sink, scrubbing the old cast iron skillet, the last dish that needed washed.

"Would you like to sit on the swing for a bit?" he asked as she wiped the table.

"Sure," she said, hoping his question was code for kissing.

Her phone buzzed, an international number. She lifted a shoulder at McKoy's quizzical look and answered, "*Bueno?*"

"Jillian. This is Mario. I need you to make a decision about Heidi. Hazel hasn't eaten all week, and she's fading fast. I want to fly in tomorrow to get her and I want you to come back down with me."

Jillian swallowed. She looked at McKoy who had finished scrubbing the skillet and had slowly turned. The narrowing of his eyes told her he'd figured out that this was a call they had dreaded. He wiped his hands on a tea towel, lifting his chin. He carefully hung the towel back up and walked out of the kitchen, through the door, and onto the back porch. Closing the door behind him.

She thought that meant he was giving her privacy to make the decision herself, without feeling pressure from him.

"She's lying down and hasn't gotten up all day..."

"I'll go," she said.

"This will not be completely legal according to the United States government, so I can't tell you exactly when I'll arrive, but sometime before dark. I'll work out the logistics."

That was fine with her. She didn't need to know details.

She bit her lip. She didn't want to lose her elephants. She loved them, and Hazel knew her, so maybe having Heidi and her both come down would be the perk that she needed.

Maybe she wouldn't need to stay down long. Trouble was she still owed money from sneaking across the border the last time. Once she left, she might never return. Those days in the desert had almost killed her.

She hung up with Mario just before someone knocked on the door.

Jillian thought about getting McKoy, but he'd probably heard the car and would be coming in soon. She walked to the door and opened it.

A tall blond stood on the step with a bottle of wine, impossibly long legs and a short skirt that showed most of them.

"I didn't know McKoy had hired a cleaning lady." The blond sniffed, brushing by her. "Where is he?"

Jillian closed the door, turning and leaning against it. McKoy came in the back door, his brows knitted together, until he saw the blond.

Jillian wasn't an expert on reading his facial expressions, but there was something that passed quickly over his features that said this woman was more than a stranger to him.

If she had to make a guess, she'd say this was his ex-fiancée. He'd just talked to her not that long ago. And Jillian knew that whatever the woman had done to McKoy, he'd never really recovered from it. Maybe it was just as well that Jillian had just agreed to leave the country.

But McKoy's eyes didn't rest on the tall blond. He barely acknowledged her. His gaze skipped past her and speared Jillian.

Like a magnet, they pulled her to him. She resisted at first. Whatever this woman wanted, she looked like a person that was used to getting her way, and Jillian didn't want to rock her boat.

But she couldn't resist McKoy and his expression. She pushed off from the door and walked across the kitchen in front of the tall woman to his side. His arm came around her and something like relief eased his features.

"Isabella, this is my girlfriend, Jillian." His voice rumbled against her side and she cherished the feeling of being tucked close. Although he probably suspected it, he didn't know for sure that she had committed to going to Brazil. There wasn't much time left for them.

Isabella's face contorted. Her fingers flexed around the bottle she carried. Finally, she gave a regal lift to her chin. "I got the job. I wanted to thank you for your character reference. I brought this as a token of my appreciation."

She held the bottle up before setting it on the table with a clank. One side of her mouth pulled back as she looked at McKoy and Jillian. "Looks like you don't need me." She swallowed, then her eyes settled on Jillian. "For what it's worth, he's a good man."

Spinning on her heel, her dress riffling around her thighs, she strode to the door and walked out.

The house was quiet after she left, like she'd taken all the life with it. Jillian didn't want to break the silence, but she felt that she owed McKoy.

"Maybe you want her." She was going to talk about leaving, about going to Brazil, about how she owed the money and couldn't try to get back in the country, didn't want to die in the desert, but she couldn't bring all those words to her lips.

Instead, she turned into McKoy and put her arms around him, tucking her head into his chest.

"No." He put his arms around her, holding her close. "You're leaving?" he asked.

"I told him I would. Hazel is down."

His arms tightened. "I wanted to tell you tonight. Todd accepted a bribe to fake the inspection failure and sell Heidi to a game preserve. They found his emails, and apparently the trail wasn't hard to follow. Although he might have gotten away with it if it hadn't been for us."

He meant them being together, she supposed. Since Todd wouldn't have had to fake the failure if McKoy hadn't helped her build that fence.

"He's being apprehended and I have the promotion." His breath huffed out. "Which doesn't seem like such a good thing if you're not going to be here."

His hands pressed down her back and pulled her closer. "Ah, Jillian. I'd give it all up and go with you. I don't care about the job, and I'd leave my country. Maybe that's crazy, but I wouldn't even have to think twice."

"But?"

His shoulders slumped and he set his forehead down on top of her head. "How can I leave Uncle Roy?"

She could not get upset at something that made complete sense. "If I can't leave Heidi, I certainly can't expect you to leave Uncle Roy. It wouldn't be right."

"I assumed that's what the phone call was about?" he asked in the quiet stillness.

"Yes. Tomorrow, sometime before dark is what he said."

"I see." His voice was low and careful. "Then tonight could be the last time I ever see you."

Her breath came out on a shaky sigh. "I still owe money for the last time I came over. I'd better pay that before I even think about—"

"No. It's too dangerous. You shouldn't have done it the first time, I definitely don't want you using the drug cartel to come back."

She leaned back a little. "I'm coming back to you. I'm not asking you to wait, and I'm not even saying I want you to. I just want you to know that when I've taken care of Hazel and Heidi, and paid my debt, I'll be coming back to you."

"I can't get money until Monday. Give me the information. I'll pay it."

Her heart froze. "I'm not putting a gringo in touch with the Mexican drug cartel. We'd both get killed."

"Then I'll wire you the money."

"No. It's my problem, I need to take care of it."

A muscle ticked in his jaw. "I'm all about taking responsibility for your problems, but not in this case. I want to be with you now, not sometime in the future. You can owe me, if that's how you want to play it, although it's not what I want."

She put her hand on his cheek and pressed closer to him. "Let's not spend our last night together arguing."

They kissed in the kitchen for a long time. They didn't need words to communicate that neither of them wanted to part. Eventually they made their way out to the porch and sat on the front porch swing until the sun came up, Jillian snuggled close with McKoy's strong arms around her.

She didn't know what he was thinking about, but she spent the night enjoying his closeness and trying to figure out some way for them to be together. Surely there was a way. But if there was, she couldn't think of it. Not one that kept the elephants safe, kept Uncle Roy in the home he loved, and allowed McKoy to keep his integrity. She needed to be legal in order for that to happen.

Still, despite the unresolved issues in her head, she enjoyed these last few hours. They could sleep tomorrow.

Finally the sky started flaming orange and pink, and it was time for Jillian to go take care of her animals.

"I can take care of your kenneled dogs until the last one is picked up," McKoy said as they cleaned out the kennels, his voice and posture as depressed as she'd ever seen it.

She showed him the information in her small office. She didn't have a computer system, just a note pad with people's and dogs' names on it. She had been charging, both for her classes and for kenneling, on a weekly basis, so there wasn't much to cancelling her classes.

McKoy had on his serious face, and she knew the dogs would all be in good hands. His integrity wouldn't allow him to do any different.

They took care of Heidi together. He stood in the back while she taught three obedience classes before lunch. Every time she looked at him, his hot gaze was following her every move. The emptiness in her chest grew and expanded until she felt like it would swallow her whole. It was torture to try to concentrate on teaching when her heart hurt like it had already been ripped from her chest.

McKoy figured whoever was coming would be late picking up the elephant, but he was wrong. A tractor-trailer showed up shortly after three. He and Jillian sat on her stoop, her slender body tucked between his legs. He had his arms wrapped around her and couldn't keep from wondering why it had taken his whole life to find his perfect match only to have her taken from him as soon as he had her. It didn't seem fair.

But life wasn't fair.

They watched as the big tractor trailer crept down the driveway. He couldn't stop his hands from fisting, but he did keep from holding onto Jillian. She'd made the decision to leave, to do what was best for the animals she loved. At the same time, he had to do right by the man who'd raised him. So she had to leave and he wasn't going to stop her, no matter how badly he might want to.

A sedan followed the truck down the lane, heading toward Jillian's house, while the truck backed into the barn.

Jillian had said that Fink and Ellie and their children were heading to a conference today, so McKoy didn't worry about any kids getting run over. Snickers was on the porch with them. Jillian had said that Fink and Ellie were taking her, as well.

He ran that all over in his mind as the car, a Lexus, came to a stop in front of the porch. A Latino man, with a big white smile, wearing a black business suit, stepped confidently out of the driver's door.

Barely glancing at McKoy, the man had eyes only for Jillian. "I would recognize you anywhere, my beautiful darling. Jillian Powel, the most stunning performer to ever work under the big top." He walked to the step, holding out his hand and taking Jillian's in his, despite McKoy's arms still being around her.

She stiffened, but allowed it. McKoy ground his teeth together. This man was not going to make her leaving less painful.

McKoy couldn't help noticing that next to the flashy car and fashionable suit, his old truck and jeans and a T-shirt looked ragged and, dare he think it, boring.

He'd already told himself that Jillian wasn't like his mother or his sisters or his fiancée, and he truly believed it, but the thought kept punching into his consciousness like hammer blows.

She wasn't leaving because he bored her. She was doing it because of her animals. But next to this charismatic man, McKoy felt boring. Jillian would have a more exciting life with him, no doubt.

Jillian stood and McKoy stood with her.

"We need to move quickly," the man said. "I'm Mario." He held a hand out to McKoy.

McKoy shook it and gave his own name. One word. Mario's handshake was firm, his eye contact direct. McKoy couldn't find anything not to like. Except the familiar and possessive way he acted toward Jillian—the hand on her shoulder, the lingering gaze on her face, the way his body invaded her space and ignored McKoy's presence.

But McKoy wouldn't let himself fight over her. She could make the decision. It wouldn't be right for him to try to force her to choose him for the next thirty minutes when she was leaving anyway. So he backed off, walking beside her, not holding her hand or keeping his arm around her as he wanted.

He opened the gate as she brought Heidi out and carried several bales of hay up the ramp of the trailer as Jillian waited and Mario talked about how Hazel was doing.

Jillian's eyes, normally full of fire and snap, were dull, and McKoy took cold comfort in that, at least.

Heidi walked right up onto the trailer. They made sure she was settled and closed the door behind her.

The driver pulled out while McKoy followed Mario and Jillian up the drive. When Mario put his arm around Jillian's shoulders, McKoy's backbone heated like red-hot metal and his chest felt like the inside of a hot air balloon. But he kept his hands at his side and stoically made each foot fall in front of the other, determined to see it through to the end.

Jillian moved away, and Mario's hand dropped. That helped ease the pressure in McKoy's chest, but he could hardly wait to be finished here, so he could go into the woods somewhere and ease the scalding rawness that scraped every nerve in his body.

It had been years since he'd felt like crying. Maybe since his parents split.

Was he doing the wrong thing by staying with Uncle Roy? It seemed like a very responsible, boring thing to do. Why couldn't he ditch any responsibility to him and follow Jillian?

But there was nothing in his character that would allow him to shove his uncle in a nursing home so he could be free to do what he wanted.

"I have a suitcase," Jillian said as they reached the porch. "McKoy will help me get it."

Mario took the hint and stayed by his car. Jillian took McKoy's hand and pulled him up the step and into her house.

He'd not been in since the day she'd burnt supper. It felt like a long time ago. But he didn't have time to look around, because as soon as the door was shut behind them, Jillian turned, grabbing his head in both hands and kissing him with a desperation that pulled every last bit of strength from his body. Everything felt weak, his knees, his legs, his lungs, but he clung to her and kissed her back, knowing it could be the last time. He kissed her straight from his soul.

Her suitcase was by the door, and when she ripped her mouth from his, with no words between them, he picked it up, clenching his jaw, and followed her out.

Chapter 20

Six Weeks Later

Jillian forked hay into the pen for Hazel and Heidi. "I always make sure there is no waste in the area where they eat," she explained to Kira, the girl David had hired to be Jillian's replacement.

Kira nodded solemnly. She'd been a fast learner, and in the week that she'd been in Brazil, she'd pretty much learned everything Jillian could teach.

Kira had worked with elephants before, which is how David had found her—working in a Mexico City zoo—and Jillian was confident that Kira loved Hazel and Heidi and would be a good companion.

David had found the money—the men Ricardo sent with Heidi had never taken it with them —and wired it to her. Jillian had been able to pay off all her debts, and she no longer owed the drug cartel.

She had enough to pay to try to get back into America, but McKoy had specifically told her he didn't want her taking that chance. She was torn. On one hand, she wanted to be back with him, but on the other, she knew he was right. It was a dangerous game, and security at the border had only increased, which did not put the cartel workers in a good mood. To say the least.

Kira took the shovel and started cleaning out the manure in the large, lavish enclosure. Jillian leaned against the fence.

Tonight Mario was driving her to the airport. His plane took off early tomorrow morning. She'd be in Mexico this time tomorrow.

She could apply for a work visa or even immigration status, but her chances of being accepted, without any kind of skill or job or secondary education was low. But that's what McKoy would want.

He'd never said he would wait for her. She hadn't asked him to. But just knowing what kind of man he was, she'd bet everything she had that he'd love her until he died. It was just the way he was. Part of the reason she loved him.

Therefore, she could afford to take her time and do it right. Not that she wanted to. Sometimes she could hardly control the irritation in her chest that made her want to start north, walking if she had to, to get to McKoy.

But it wasn't the best way, and she was determined to try to do it right. This time.

Kira got done cleaning the pen, putting the shovel away and taking the wheelbarrow over to the waste pile. Kira also had experience with horses and ostriches, both of which Mario had.

As Jillian watched, Mario met Kira by the horse pens. They must have planned to go riding together, because Mario was dressed in his riding clothes—shiny boots and carrying a crop. It hadn't taken him long to get the hint that she didn't want him touching her, even though their culture was much more touchy-feely than American culture. The only hands that felt right to her were McKoy's.

The weight of a hand fell on her shoulder. Perfect. Like she'd imagined it. Only...she put her fingers up, touching rough flesh.

Her heart stuttered as her eyes popped open.

She spun, coming face to face with deep blue eyes. His blond hair was a little longer, but his shoulders were just as broad and his face just as handsome.

She didn't wait to talk, but threw herself into his arms, reaching up to kiss him before he could even say hello.

His arms slid around her, but he didn't allow the kiss to last long. His lips were turned up. "No. I can't think when you kiss me."

"We don't need to think. Just feel happy."

"I need my brain." His words were choppy, like her kiss had already affected him. "I need to figure out how to convince you to marry me."

She blinked. Then smiled. "Yes." However he'd gotten here, whatever he'd had to do, she wasn't going to make the same mistake as the last time, thinking that his proposal wasn't romantic enough or whatever her problem had been. If he was mentioning marriage, she was saying yes.

He laughed. "I thought it might be harder than that."

"Is that what took you so long?"

"No. I booked my plane ticket yesterday, the second I got my passport." He looked out over the enclosure. "It looks like Hazel and Heidi are doing well."

"Oh. Yeah." They were. She'd forgotten he didn't even have a passport. "Marriage? How? What?" She had so many questions and they all jumbled in her head.

He hadn't stopped smiling, and other than to look at the elephants, he hadn't taken his eyes off her. His hand ran down her hair. "I talked to a lawyer. He said our best bet was for me to marry you in Mexico, then apply at the US consulate for residency for you."

"How long?" What about his job? Uncle Roy?

"I don't know. He couldn't say. They might not give it." His broad shoulders moved up. "Gator's mother said you'd helped Avery take care of her when she had cancer, so she was moving in with Uncle Roy, to be with him. However long it takes us to get you back in the US. Legally. So you can stay. Forever." His eyes drilled down into hers. There was nothing she wanted more than to be with him forever.

"If they won't let you in, I'll apply to live in Mexico. Or somewhere. We'll find somewhere to be together."

"Really?"

"I don't care where. I truly don't. The only thing I care about is being with you."

Her eyes widened at his words. Her hands gripped him tighter. "I love you."

"I haven't heard that nearly enough." His gripped loosened, and he bent a knee on the dry ground, pulling a small box out of his pocket. "Jillian. I love you. More than anything. Marry me, please?" He opened the box.

A small ruby, surrounded by diamonds winked up at her. The ring was breathtaking, but she didn't care.

"Yes." A thousand times yes.

He slipped it on her finger, and stood.

"What about your job?" she asked, searching his face, hoping he wouldn't regret all the sacrifices he'd made.

"I told them I was taking some personal time. It's possible Louie will stay for a while and see if I come back. Maybe the supervisor position will still be there." He kissed her hand, then cupped her face. "I don't care. I'm proud to be an American. I enjoy my job. But I love you. When I think that way, decisions are easy." He grinned. Wolfishly. "Now, do you suppose I can talk my fiancée into kissing her world traveler?"

It was a long kiss.

Epilogue

Zane, Abe, Beck, and Cash.

Fink and Ellie's kitchen, three months later, nine 'o clock at night.

Zane Wilder sat in Fink and Ellie Finkenbinder's kitchen, a thick portfolio of plans, estimates, and diagrams lying on the table in front of him. Normally this was not his area. His brother, Abe, was the architect and the one that normally closed on all the big deals. Unfortunately he, along with Beck and Cash, were still in California finishing up their last project.

Zane owned an excavation company, and he'd been done with that job for over a week. He was much more comfortable sitting in the cab of his twenty-ton dozer, nicknamed Fat Alice, than he was sitting here at the table, hoping to ink a multimillion-dollar deal for his brothers and himself.

Of course, the fact that he was back in Gail's hometown might have a little something to do with the uncomfortable itchiness in his chest.

"Thanks for meeting us so late," Fink said as he set a cup of coffee down in front of Ellie before taking his own seat and putting his coffee on the table.

"No problem. For a job this big, we can make some concessions." Happy to hear that his voice didn't shake, Zane returned Gator's smile across the table. He'd gone to elementary school with Gator before his family imploded and the Mahoneys took him in. Ab, Beck, and Cash treated him just like a fourth brother, even if their parents had never officially adopted him.

Gator leaned back and put a big arm around his wife, Avery. Her pink nails and quirky outfit contrasted with Gator's dark, brooding largeness, but it was obvious from the way they looked at each other that they were wildly in love. "It's better this way," Gator said. "If we do it before the kids go to bed, it's hard to concentrate."

"And we'd have to say everything twice," Ellie added. She exchanged a knowing smile with her daughter, Harper, who sat with her husband, Wyatt, on the other side of the table. They'd come up from Chile, where they were running a resort similar to the one that was in the plans on the table in front of Zane. It was Zane's understanding that Wyatt had something to do with the financing and that he and his wife were going to be operating the resort in Pennsylvania once it was completed.

"Well, the main reason we waited was because we thought Jillian and McKoy would be getting in tonight." Harper snuggled more firmly into Wyatt's side, her hand on her protruding stomach. His arm holding her close.

"I knew McKoy in school," Zane said.

"He and Jillian were married in Mexico a few months ago. Jillian's been waiting for the US embassy to approve her visa, which they've done, and they were heading home early this morning." Fink took a small sip of his coffee.

"Jillian texted me an hour ago and said they were on their way," Avery said, her bracelets sparkling in the overhead kitchen light.

"How much time do you have, Zane?" Fink asked. "Jillian has worked to keep things on the farm going, plus she's part of the family. I'd like to involve her, and now McKoy, if we can. Can we wait a few more minutes?"

Zane shrugged, resisting the urge to tug at the collar of the unfamiliar polo shirt he wore. He was used to worn T-shirts. "I have all night." His brothers were depending on him to land the deal for all of them. Not just Abe, who already had the architectural contract, but Cash expected to use his construction company to build the buildings, and Beck wanted the contract for the electrical systems, along with all the HVAC work.

They had everything wrapped up in one bid, as they did with every project they worked on together, now sitting on the table in front of Zane.

Fink and Ellie had given their verbal agreement, after looking at other bids and giving the Mahoney brothers precedent over the rest because of them being a local family, although their bundled bid was the lowest, too.

Still, Zane felt the pressure of needing to perform and not let his adopted brothers down. He owed the Mahoney family a debt he could never pay. He'd not been perfect over the years, Gail being a case in point, but the Mahoneys didn't know about her.

"If we'd have done this in the morning—" Fink started, but he was interrupted by the door opening.

A dark-haired beauty, slender and graceful, walked in. A tall, broad-shouldered blond dude followed her. The couples at the table turned, and everything went quiet before pandemonium broke out.

Zane was the only one left at the table as McKoy and—Zane assumed it was Jillian with him—were surrounded, hugged, and grilled on their stay in Mexico, their trip home, their marriage, and Jillian's visa.

It was a good twenty minutes before they dragged McKoy and Jillian to the table and sat them down beside Zane. At that point Zane had heard so much about them, he knew their history almost as well as he knew his own.

And he was happy for them. Really. They looked totally in love as they smiled into each other's eyes. Obviously, with Jillian's accent, their backgrounds were different, but the way they cuddled and laughed together, the way they seemed to know what the other was thinking, the way they touched, both with their hands and their gazes, it was obvious they were meant for each other.

Zane could have had that with Gail. But he'd messed everything up until the only thing left for him to do was leave.

Through the years that had gone by, he'd become successful. Maybe not in the way her dad considered success, with a college degree and a white collar to wear to work every day, but financially successful. He might not be a pillar of society, but protective mamas didn't shove their young daughters behind their backs when he strolled into town. Not anymore.

Maybe it was just first love. Or maybe it was truly that Gail was his soulmate. Whatever. He couldn't get interested in the women who wanted him now.

As much as he wanted to be the other half of a happy couple like the ones around the table, there was only one girl who'd ever felt like she was the one who would make him whole.

And he'd burned that bridge.

If he got this job, he'd be working for several months in Love. Maybe he'd see Gail. Not that there could ever be anything between them after what he did, but just so maybe he could see that she wasn't the angel that his dreams made her out to be.

No woman could be that perfect.

Enjoy this preview of Book One of the Baxter Boys series, *Always With You*, just for you!

Always With You

Chapter 1

Cassidy Kimball stood on the cement sidewalk and faced the red brick Pennsylvania state penitentiary building. Hot July sunlight glinted off the razor wire that looped in circles at the top and beside the chain-link fence. Off to the right, the circular guard house, with its tinted windows, glared down at the parched brown and empty exercise yard.

Her stomach twisted like mangled metal in a car accident.

It could have been her on the inside. Not here, of course. But somewhere.

She glanced at her watch before dragging her clammy hands down her skirt. *Please, God, don't let my makeup melt before he walks out.* A simple request; she shouldn't care what her makeup looked like, although right now, it felt like much-needed armor. Plus, she'd learned the hard way to be thankful for little things.

And big things. Like not serving the ten-year prison sentence for vehicular homicide that should have been hers after she T-boned a car with Torque Baxter's pickup when she was nineteen. Nope, she didn't serve it. Because Torque was serving, had served, it for her.

Hot and turbulent doubt swirled in her stomach. Would he see what she had become and think his sacrifice had been worth it?

Part of her wanted to announce her sacrifices to him, to tell him of her charity work and the people she helped. That he had played the gallant knight in shining armor to her Cowardly Lion, but that it had not been in vain. Part of her wanted him to see it for himself. All of her craved his approval. Or maybe just his forgiveness.

Swallowing the nerves that clenched her throat, Cassidy twisted the delicate linked gold of her wristwatch. Any minute now. Would she still recognize him? Of course, she would. The question was, would he recognize all that she had done as a tiny down payment on the huge debt she owed him?

She reached the same conclusion she had every day for the last ten years. There was nothing she could do to pay back her monstrous obligation. There was no way to atone for the cowardice that she had shown. How could she have been so yellow?

When he'd seen the passengers in the other car, when he'd known what the consequences were going to be, he'd never wavered. His brown eyes had been steady and level as he said, "Get out of here and don't look back. You don't know anything about this." She hadn't understood at first what he was going to do. Still shaken from the accident, she'd not really been thinking straight. But she hadn't needed her brain to be fully functioning to know that she was in deep trouble. She'd already been fighting the urge to run. His command had prompted her to do what she subconsciously wanted to. "Hurry, before anyone comes."

Then, he hadn't accepted her calls, hadn't graced her visits with his presence, hadn't used the money she deposited in his account. Her letters returned unopened, and her emails disappeared into the prison of cyberspace. She didn't know, couldn't know, what he thought or felt.

She assumed he hated her.

A bead of sweat trickled down her temple. Her watch chain snapped under her shaking fingers. She shoved the broken links into her clutch.

Her hands stilled as the prison door opened. The jaws of a monster spitting out its prey. Prey she had fed it.

A man, tall and straight, strode out into the sunlight. Her eyes devoured him. Same casual arrogance dressed in jeans and a t-shirt. Same confident walk, with only a slight limp. The limp was her fault, too. With his slim build, Torque would never be bulky, but she could see the t-shirt that probably fit him when he first walked into this building as an almost-eighteen-year-old now stretched tight over shoulders that had widened and filled out.

Cassidy bit her lip and lifted her chin, taking a deep breath to calm the cramping of her stomach and disguise the curl of heat that came to life in her chest. Torque had always had that effect on her. She pushed the feeling aside and channeled her inner upper-crust snob—the only defense that had ever come close to working against the elemental pull that Torque exerted on her.

The last words that man had said to her were, "Shut up, Cassidy." Now, she intended to get one question answered. Then she had to figure out how to pay him back. What did ten years of a man's life cost?

Torque floated above the sidewalk, taking in big lungfuls of the sweetest smelling air in the country. Same air that he'd been breathing for the last decade, but it smelled different on this side of the fence. Felt different, too. He wanted to lie belly-down and kiss the ground. He resisted the urge.

Instead he exalted in the unchaining of his spirit, in the freedom and openness that surrounded him, in the beautiful blue sky, in the purple mountains of his home state unobscured by fences or bars.

His stomach rumbled.

A small talon of anxiety poked his rib. He'd have to find his own meal tonight. After years of his basic needs being met on a schedule with no thought of his own being necessary... He pushed the thought away. He'd taken care of himself for years before he went up. It was a privilege to do so again. He couldn't think of it any other way. He certainly was not going to worry about it. There were things that, to him, were more important than eating, anyway.

Before he'd been locked up, he'd been well on his way to his goal of owning his own diesel garage. But technology had moved on without him. A few outdated Popular Mechanics weren't enough to update his knowledge of emissions standards and computerized motors. Still, surely there was some diesel garage that would hire a hard worker and a quick learner. With a rap sheet.

First things first. He scanned the sidewalk for his brother Turbo or at least a monster pickup that would be Turbo's latest project. All he saw was a slender woman in a slim skirt with miles of legs reaching down to impossibly high heels. She stood at the T in the sidewalk. Long brown hair streaked with blond. Big shades. Not Turbo.

He didn't allow his eyes to linger. Beautiful women had been few and far between in the lockup. But he wasn't going there, although his eyes were drawn to this one like air to the intake valve. He had a life to put back together first.

She stood with one hip jutted out. A hand with shiny red nails rested on it. Her whole bearing screamed money and class.

Most definitely not for him.

He altered his direction, aiming to give her a good ten-foot birth on the right without being obvious about avoiding her. His infatuation with one such girl was how he had landed in the pen to begin with.

Infatuation.

No. Chivalry.

Whatever. It would have driven him to step between her and a bullet. That would have been a heck of a lot faster than what he actually did, which was put himself in her place, and *she had allowed it*. He'd told her to. He'd volunteered to do it. He'd kept his word and protected her through it all. That was great. But his sacrificing days were done. Not going down that road again.

The woman casually removed her shades.

Torque's heart rammed to a stop the way a rod shot through the side of a block kills an engine.

Cassidy.

What was she doing here? All his body systems slammed into overdrive.

He clenched his jaw and kept walking. He'd be ready to face her when he had put his life back together. When he could meet her on equal footing, and she no longer looked down her cute, rich-girl's nose at him.

Who was he kidding? Like he'd ever be good enough.

Turbo had to be around here somewhere. *Please, God.* Another sweep of the visitors' parking lot revealed only a low-slung, red sports car.

Mere feet from Cassidy, he surrendered to the inevitable and stopped. Her scent overwhelmed him. Exotic fruit. The memory of a hot summer night slammed into him. Radio on. Cruising. Country air blowing into his truck and tangling with the incense of the girl next to him. Suddenly the urge to turn and run surged through him. Back into the prison, back where the smell of perfume and the twitch of a lip didn't turn his brain to mush and make him do the stupidest thing a man had ever done for a woman, back to where his brain and heart weren't engaged in all-out warfare and where it would be easy to remember the only smart choice he needed to make: stay away from Cassidy.

Those soft red lips, the ones he'd dreamed about for years, the ones he'd heard later that same night scream in terror, opened. "Why'd you take my place, Torque?"

Torque schooled his features, refusing to allow the longing her voice elicited to show on his face. Rich, yet friendly, living in her mansion on the hill, Cassidy had infatuated him since this poor, trailer-park trash saw her in the kindergarten lunch line. He had plenty of experience in shoving that magnetic attraction aside and pretending indifference.

He didn't have to fake the bitterness.

"Didn't hear you on the witness stand contradicting my story."

"You told me to shut up."

"Has to be the first time in your life you listened to anyone." Was that hurt that flickered across her features? Couldn't be. Not Cassidy. Tough as tempered steel. "You've got a mouth, and I've never seen you afraid to use it."

"My dad wouldn't let me."

Torque snorted. What a line of crap. "Your dad wouldn't let you ride with me either. But that didn't stop you." Heat spread up his side as he remembered how she felt snuggled up against him on the bench seat, her hair whipping in the wind, her laughing eyes and flashing teeth grinning up at him. Her hand clenching his leg. For that one short ride, he'd forgotten that she was rich and he poor and that their futures, headed in completely opposite directions, would never merge into one.

But where he'd been since then wasn't so easily wiped away, and he allowed his heart to harden. She was tempered steel. He was titanium. She would break first. This time.

"After the accident, it was different. He wouldn't let me out of his sight until you..." Her voice trailed off, and she looked away.

"Until I was locked up?" he asked with a sardonic lift to his brow. He wanted to close the step between them and take her in his arms. Not that she needed it or wanted it. It was simply the effect she always had on him, like there was a vulnerability to her that no one but him could see, and it brought out every protective instinct in his body. He hated himself for it. He hated her even more.

"Yeah," she whispered. A breeze lifted her hair, showcasing the elegant curve of her neck. She turned her head, and he looked away.

"Plus, you had given the police a lie. I wasn't going to contradict that without talking to you." Her chin tilted. "You wouldn't talk to me."

She visited the jail once, where he was being held, unable to make bail. Strutting down the corridor in her designer clothes

amid catcalls a...
belonged on a Par...
ing like him, surroun...
nals locked up in that dum...
away, refusing to speak to her. ...
impulsive decision he made the n...
belong in there. And as much as he c...
loved her or hated her, he could at least pr...

His dad might have been a lousy paren... ...se
child-naming skills, who eventually ran off, but n... ... and
grandmother had instilled a rock-solid code of ethics n... ...s brain.
Women deserve protection. They might not want it. They might
not need it. Still. A woman nurtures, a man protects. And with
Cassidy, and the hold she had on his over-hormoned teenaged
brain...heck, he hadn't used his brain at all to make that decision.

But with that choice—the choice to become a convicted criminal—went the last hope he harbored that he might eventually be
able to knock on the door of her mansion and speak to her father
as an equal, seeking and receiving permission to date his daughter.

He couldn't let her see his weakness. He couldn't articulate his
reasons then, and he wasn't sure he wanted to now. He changed
the subject instead. "Well, it's been fun, getting reacquainted and
all, but Turbo's gonna be here any minute." Torque stepped toward
the parking lot.

"He's not coming."

Torque stopped midstride. His stomach sank like water in oil, a
slow, graceful, unstoppable dive to his feet.

"I told him I'd bring you home." She spoke to his back.

Turbo owned his own truck and was busy, of course, but Torque
hadn't thought that would abandon him to Cassidy. Of course,
Turbo didn't know how twisted his feelings for her were, either.

Steeling himself against the idea of spending the next three
hours cooped up in a car with Cassidy, he turned back. "The last
time I rode with you isn't in my top ten best memories."

imagination.

...er. Not really. And he didn't hate her. But he ...insist that he drive, wanted to dominate her because ...he inferiority complex she always brought out in him, but his license was long expired. Just one thing on a long list of things for him to take care of.

Cassidy stepped closer and put one shiny red fingernail on his chest where it scalded like acid through his t-shirt. He couldn't have moved or looked away from her blue-black gaze even if his shirt had incinerated from his body.

"I asked you why you lied. Why you took my place. Why you served the time that should have been mine."

He stared over her shoulder. There was no way he was going there.

Her minty breath flowed over his face. "Torque, I owe you. I don't know what ten years are worth, I'm not sure you can put a price tag on them, but I have to do something to pay you."

This obligation that she felt didn't sit right. The feelings that he wanted from her were much deeper and more intimate.

He didn't want her to owe him, *he wanted her to love him*.

Stepping away from her dagger of a finger, he started walking again. "I don't want anything from you."

"Torque..." Her heels clicked on the pavement as she hurried after him. The red sports car was hers. Had to be.

The "Bus Stop" sign caught his eye. He fingered the small amount of money in his pocket. A small sliver of anxiety slipped through him. It had been so long since he'd done anything for himself. Getting on a bus, paying the fare... Another burst of anxiety, thicker and heavier, tore through his chest.

Suddenly the fresh air, the wide-open space, the looming mountains in the distance, all seemed too big, too much, too threatening.

He set his jaw, refusing to give in to the sudden insecurity. He wouldn't ride with Cassidy. He'd take the bus, prove that he could do it.

"Torque!"

He swung around, realizing that Cassidy had said his name several times, and he'd been so caught up in the grip of anxiety and borderline panic, he'd not even heard her. He hadn't expected to have that kind of trouble adjusting to life on the outside.

Setting his feet, he crossed his arms over his chest. "Yeah?" he asked, grateful his voice didn't crack and hoping his face didn't show the anxiety that still curled in his chest.

"This is my car." She indicated the beat-up dark blue clunker beside him.

Surprise shot through him. He tried to cover it, but his eyes ripped back to her, the skyscraper heels, the fancy blouse and classic skirt. The perfect hair and makeup. It all screamed money and class. But the car?

"I'm taking the bus." He turned. Whatever her deal, he really didn't want any part of it. If he kept telling himself that, he might start to believe it.

"Torque, wait."

He stopped but didn't turn.

"Listen, I know you're angry for what happened..."

"Not at what happened. And I'm not angry," he said through clenched teeth.

"Great imitation," she said, half under her breath.

He spun. Couldn't stop himself from taking a step toward her, reaching out, and grabbing her forearm. "I had enough time in the last ten years to figure out I was just a toy for you. Something you played with when you were bored with your high-society life. I get it." He dropped her arm like it had erupted in hot grease. Her skin felt soft and warm and alive under his fingers. Fingers that hadn't seen much human contact and definitely not the softness of a woman in the last ten years. He shut his mouth, clenched his fist, and stomped off.

"I'm your sponsor."

He skidded to a stop. Turned slowly. "No," he said drawing the word out even as he racked his brain for where he might be wrong. "I served my whole sentence. Every day of it. I'm out, free and clean. No parole. No stipulations."

"It's a new program. Officially called the Reintegration into Society Sponsorship Program, it's designed to help people who have been in prison for a while readjust to society, find or keep a job, update on the latest technology, brush up their skill sets, that type of thing. It pairs a professional with a former, uh, inmate."

He smirked as she stumbled over the word. Like she didn't know what to call him. "Ex-con. Pairs a 'professional,'" he said it in a jeering tone, "with an ex-con." Then he snorted at the irony. "Do they know they paired this ex-con with the 'professional' who should have been in prison in the first place?"

"No." Her tone was small, and he felt instant guilt. It had always been his intention to protect her, not hurt her.

He sighed. "I supposed that's what the meeting they told me I had to attend tomorrow is about?"

"Yes. It's a small program, just starting. There are eight pairs, including us."

"So, let me get this straight. You've kept up with diesel mechanics over the last ten years, and you're going to help me catch up and land a job?"

The last time, her tone had been affected, but now, for the first time, her confident carriage seemed to wilt. "It wasn't very fair of me to ask to be paired with you, was it?"

She had asked to be paired with him. To torture him? To rub in his face that he was an ex-con and she wasn't? Or, worse, out of pity?

"This isn't mandatory for me."

"No. Not for you, since you're not out on parole. But," she tilted her proud head, and her eyes almost seemed to plead. "if you were to ever get in any kind of trouble again, this would look good when you came up before the judge."

"Lady, maybe you haven't figured this out, but when that judge looks at me, all he sees is street trash that's better off out of society and behind bars."

"He's wrong."

He wasn't going to fall for her lies. Not a second time. Once, he'd believed she'd seen more in him than anyone else, that he could be successful and climb out of the gutter he'd been born into, where no one expected him to do more than get an entry-level position in some kind of manual labor job and keep it until he retired. Nothing wrong with that, but Cassidy had made him think he could be more.

He could be. He knew it. And he didn't need her to help.

"I'm not planning on getting into trouble again."

"You didn't plan this, either."

He shrugged. She was right about that.

"Listen. I might be able to help, but I need you to do this program."

"Help?" he said derisively. "Like you helped me ten years ago?"

"You told me to leave. If you had given any indication that you wanted anything from me, I would have done everything I could to do what you wanted."

"Big words. Actions don't back 'em up."

"You wouldn't talk to me, wouldn't accept my mail..."

He held a hand up. "Enough."

"You keep acting like this was my fault."

"It was."

Her lips pursed together, and she looked away. He should have felt satisfaction, but he only felt the nagging sense of guilt. Guilt for hurting her. Never mind the last ten years. Guess his heart had missed that part. It had always been on her side.

"You're the one who stole my truck," he said roughly.

"It was hardly stealing."

True. He would have given her his truck to go along with his heart, of course. The problem was he should have taught her how to drive it.

He fingered the money in his pocket. It was all he had in the world. But he wasn't getting in a car with Cassidy. He could work. He could fight. And he'd never quit. But she was his weakness. Always had been. If he were going to get out of the hole he was in now, he needed to keep his distance. She could derail his good intentions with one small touch of her hand.

Once more, he turned to go.

"I'll give you a ride."

"The bus is safer." It was a slam, and she flinched, which did not make him feel better.

She lifted her head, like she was ready to take it on the other cheek. "But you'll come to the meeting tomorrow?"

He stopped but didn't turn around. The rumbling of a motor sounded in the distance. His ride was about to arrive. "I'll think about it." He shouldn't go. Should protect himself with everything he had, but chances were he hadn't learned a thing in the pen, and he'd be there, just because he'd see Cassidy, and he'd never been able to resist that.

Pick up your copy of *Always With You* by Jessie Gussman today!

A Gift from Jessie

View this code through your smart phone camera to be taken to a page where you can download a FREE ebook when you sign up to get updates from Jessie Gussman! Find out why people say, "Jessie's is the only newsletter I open and read" and "You make my day brighter. Love, love, love reading your newsletters. I don't know where you find time to write books. You are so busy living life. A true blessing." and "I know from now on that I can't be drinking my morning coffee while reading your newsletter – I laughed so hard I sprayed it out all over the table!"